Forever ~~waiting~~ For You

D.E. Haggerty

Copyright © 2022 D.E. Haggerty

All rights reserved.

D.E. Haggerty asserts the moral right to be identified as the author of this work.

ISBN: 9798812084776

Forever For You is a work of fiction. The names, characters, places, and incidents portrayed in it are the product of the author's imagination. Any resemblance to actual persons, living or dead, events or locations is entirely coincidental.

All rights reserved. No part of this publication may be reproduced, stored in a retrieval system, or transmitted, in any form or by any means, electronic, mechanical, photocopying, recording or otherwise, without the prior permission of the author.

No portion of this book may be reproduced in any form without written permission from the publisher or author, except as permitted by U.S. copyright law.

Also by D.E. Haggerty

My Forever Love
Just For Forever
Stay For Forever
Only Forever
Meet Disaster
Meet Not
Meet Dare
Meet Hate
Bragg's Truth
Bragg's Love
Perfect Bragg
Bragg's Match
Bragg's Christmas
How to Date a Rockstar
How to Love a Rockstar
How to Fall For a Rockstar
How to be a Rockstar's Girlfriend
How to Catch a Rockstar
A Hero for Hailey
A Protector for Phoebe

A Soldier for Suzie
A Fox for Faith
A Christmas for Chrissie
A Valentine for Valerie
A Love for Lexi
About Face
At Arm's Length
Hands Off
Knee Deep
Molly's Misadventures

Chapter 1

Foul Play – forcing a woman who you know has a crush on you to be in your presence and then ignoring her crush on you

"Are you cheating on me, Ash?"

At the sound of Rowan's deep voice, every single nerve ending in my body lights up until I'm a bomb of feelings in danger of exploding any second now. *Don't turn around, Ashlyn. Don't turn around. Do. Not. Turn. Around.* And…of course, I turn around. I never was any good at following orders even when I'm the one giving them.

When my gaze lands on Rowan, my body begins to vibrate with the desire to throw myself at him. It's a desire I've been wrestling with since I was a freshman in high school when my crush on the six-foot-five-inch football player became a burning desire. And who can blame me?

Rowan's body should be splashed across the cover of every men's fitness magazine. Preferably while he's wearing as little clothing as possible. His shoulders are broad, and his hips are narrow. And I know the former professional athlete is hiding miles upon miles of muscles under those clothes. Muscles my tongue would love to explore.

But it isn't his body my fifteen-year-old self fell for. Nor is it the kind face or the sparkling brown eyes. It isn't even the lips always kicked up in a half smile.

No, my idiot teenage self fell for him when he rescued me. With my birthday falling in October, I was the youngest kid in my class. Everyone in my freshmen class loved to remind me of the fact by teasing me with the nickname 'baby'. Needless to say, I hate the word baby.

One day I decided I was done with the teasing. I was going to show that bitch Meadow I wasn't a baby. And I was going to show her with my fists. I managed to get one shot in before she pinned me to the ground and began scratching my arms and pulling on my hair.

Rowan arrived on the scene – my shining knight in football pads. He hauled Meadow off of me and dragged me to the nearest restroom where he proceeded to clean up the cuts on my arms with more gentleness than a man his size should have. I've been devoted to him ever since.

"I asked if you're cheating on me, Ash," Rowan says and brings me out of my daydream of sliding my fingers through his hair.

I narrow my eyes at him. "My name is Ashlyn. No one calls me Ash."

The left side of his lips kicks up in a smirk. "I do."

And him calling me a name no one else uses caused me to think he was finally noticing me as someone other than his friend's little sister. But Rowan made it perfectly clear he doesn't consider me as more than a sister he needs to protect at the parade last week.

Which is when I initiated Project Ashlyn Will Get Her Ass Over Rowan Now. How's it going thus far? Well, I'm standing on the sidewalk outside of *Clove's Coffee Corner* drooling over the object of my every desire. In other words, week one of the plan is a failure. Me and plans aren't the best of friends.

"Not anymore you don't," I insist. "The name is Ashlyn. Learn it. Use it. Or don't use it. Whatever."

I go for nonchalance. Considering how my voice is growling, I don't think I succeed.

Rowan raises his hands in surrender. "Sorry, Ashlyn." He emphasizes the second syllable and I want to smack him. "But you haven't answered my question."

Question. He asked a question? When? I cock my hip and place my hand on it.

"What question?"

"Why are you cheating on me?"

Cheating on him? I've never had Rowan. How could I possibly cheat on him? What idiot would dare to cheat on this man? Not this girl. I'd covet and cherish him and ensure he knew how special he is.

He nods toward *Clove's Coffee Corner*. Oh.

For the past year since I've been home after graduating from college, I've gone to *Bake Me Happy*, Rowan's bakery, pretty much every day. His donuts are to die for. To. Die. For. As my more than generous behind can attest to.

But step one of the get over Rowan plan was to stop dropping by his bakery every day hoping he'll notice I'm no longer a little girl in need of saving from some bully named Meadow. Thus, my coffee from Clove's place today.

"Her coffee's better," I claim and watch as every single muscle in Rowan's body tenses. I think I hit a nerve. I bite my lip to stop the smile from escaping and stretching across my face.

"What did you say?"

"You heard me. Clove makes the best dang coffee in Winter Falls," I say much louder than necessary.

"Prove it. In front of me and everyone else."

Everyone else? I scan the area and realize the nosy citizens of Winter Falls are surrounding us while eavesdropping on our conversation. They don't bother pretending they weren't listening. Not in Winter Falls. You have to pass a test to prove you're a busy body before you can live in this town. I wish I were joking.

"Bring it." I've never backed down from a dare and I'm not about to now either.

"Blind taste test!" someone hollers.

Rowan grabs my upper arm and drags me down the street. I try to wrestle free, but my efforts are half-hearted at best. Why would I fight his hold when my biggest desire for the past eight years has been to feel his hands on me?

We gather quite the following as we march. I notice my sisters, Aspen, Ellery, Lilac, and Juniper, in the crowd. Shouldn't they be at work on Monday morning? Ellery and Lilac wave while Juniper gives me a thumbs-up and Aspen winks at me. Naturally, my sisters know about my 'Rowan obsession' as they refer to it.

When we enter *Bake Me Happy*, a table is already set up in the middle of the bakery. Of course, it is. The grapevine in this town is faster than a goat rushing off when you've accidentally left the fence open. It was an accident. I'm not my animal-loving sister, Juniper, who thinks animals should be free to roam wherever they want.

Rowan presses me into a chair, and Aspen steps forward with a blindfold.

"Where did you get a blindfold from?"

She waggles her eyebrows. "Do you really want to know?"

No, I don't. Aspen recently reunited with her childhood love and she's all rainbows and butterflies. And I'm not jealous at all. Not. At. All.

She fits the blindfold on me and ties it behind my head before primping my hair.

"What are you doing?" I mumble to her.

"Making you pretty."

"Don't tell me you've joined the matchmaking committee."

There isn't really a matchmaking committee. It's actually a bunch of old women who enjoy sticking their noses in other people's love lives. I assumed being the youngest West sister at twenty-three would save me from their matchmaking schemes for a few years. But I have the feeling I was wrong.

"I've got ten dollars on Rowan's coffee," Aspen exclaims as she steps away from me.

Ah, yes. The other favorite past time of the people in Winter Falls. Betting on any and everything.

I cross my arms over my chest. "Are we going to do this thing or what? I've got things to do, places to be."

"Because you have five-hundred jobs. I wish you'd settle down," my mom grumbles.

Great. Here we go again. The 'pick on Ashlyn's life plans'-hour has arrived.

"Let her be, Ruby. You didn't exactly stick to your life plan," Radiance, Mom's best friend, says.

Radiance is also Lyric's mother. Lyric as in Aspen's fiancé. I wouldn't be surprised if Radiance and Mom planned for Aspen and Lyric to fall in love from the moment they both conceived their bundles of joy.

"Love conquers all," Mom sings. She probably has the goofy expression she always gets when she's thinking about Dad on her face, too.

My parents have been married for thirty-three years and are still sickening in love. I blame them for all my romantic notions. Couldn't they be similar to my college friends' parents and fight and bicker all the time? No, they have to be best friends and lovey-dovey all the time. What kind of an example are they?

"Here we go," Clove says before I hear the sound of a coffee cup being placed on the table. "No peeking."

"Peeking? I couldn't peek even if I tried. I seriously don't want to know what my sister uses this blindfold for."

"I assume it's for romantic liaisons," my other sister, Lilac, says. Lilac is Ms. Scientist. Until recently, I didn't think she knew what sex was. She proved me wrong there.

"Quiet down everyone." Rowan whistles and the crowd immediately shuts up. "Ashlyn has agreed to prove once and for all how my coffee is better than Clove's."

"Wait a minute! I didn't agree to anything of the sort."

"Yes, you did." I can hear the smirk in his voice. Jerk.

"Let's do this." The sooner this is over, the sooner I can escape from Mr. You're Like a Sister To Me's presence.

I pat the table until I find a cup of coffee. I lift it to my face and inhale the scent of sweet, sweet caffeine. And coffee beans and whatever else they put in coffee. I take a sip and sigh. This is good. Really, really good.

I set the cup down and search the table until my hands land on the other cup. I repeat the smelling and tasting. This cup is amazing as well.

"Do I have to pick one or the other?"

"Bwak. Bwak."

Juniper makes chicken sounds. She's probably flapping her arms and pretending they're wings, too. I wasn't kidding about her being an animal freak. I genuinely think she likes animals more than people, which makes her job at the Wildlife Refuge outside of town a perfect fit.

I try both of the coffees again. They're both delicious, but one has a slight caramel taste to it. And I do love me some caramel.

"This one." I raise the cup and cheers erupt in the crowd.

Rowan whips the blindfold off of my face. He beams down at me. "I'll expect you at the bakery tomorrow."

Damn him to decaf hell and back. I must have chosen his coffee.

Without saying another word, I stand and walk away. How in the world am I supposed to get over the man when he performs stunts to force me to be near him every day?

Chapter 2

Call an audible – to improvise the next step in a plan because your sisters are too busy teasing you to help planning

"Hear ye, hear ye. The first meeting of the Mystery of the Black Hat Bandit's Missing Loot is now in session," I yell to make myself heard above my sisters yapping away.

"Wait. What? I thought we were here to discuss you and Rowan." Aspen wiggles her eyebrows.

I groan. "There is no me and Rowan."

"I don't know why not. You like him. He's hot. What are you waiting for?"

Waiting for? Is she serious? I've spent eight years of my life waiting for the man to realize I'm not some little girl. I'm done waiting.

Ellery screams and jumps to her feet. "What the hell is that thing?" She waves her hands toward the hallway.

"It's not a thing. It's Dale. The chipmunk Juniper promised she wouldn't adopt," I snarl at said sister.

Juniper widens her eyes and bats her lashes in fake misery. "You didn't seriously expect me to abandon him at *Unleashed*, did you?"

Unleashed is the pet store in town. It's owned by Forest who doesn't understand not all animals should be pets. Juniper and him are thick as thieves despite Forest being old enough to be her grandfather and his penchant for forgetting to wear pants.

My sister never met an animal she didn't love. Including rattlesnakes. I had to put my foot down before she brought one home. Sometimes I wonder what possesses me to live with my animal obsessed sister. And then I remember the magic word. It's not please. No, this magic word is money.

When I came back to town after graduating from college, I assumed I'd live with my parents until my business was up and running. All it took was one Sunday of waking up early to grab a cup of coffee only to discover my parents in a compromising position in the kitchen and I was done. I moved in with Juniper and her two-thousand pets the next day.

"What I think is he's a chipmunk," I tell my animal lover sister. "Why can't you let him free? You don't seem to mind letting Phoenix's goats free."

She frowns. "Phoenix's goats know where they live. They come home at the end of the day. Dale, on the other hand, has never lived in the great outdoors. He wouldn't survive."

And this is why she has the aforementioned two-thousand pets. She thinks it's her job to save all the animals in the world.

"Whatever. Let's get this meeting started."

Lilac raises her hand. "Why are we having a meeting regarding the Mystery of the Black Hat Bandit's Missing Loot?"

The mystery began a couple of months ago when Aspen returned home because her life was falling apart. She got conned into helping Saffron at the bookstore and while she was nosing around in the back room, she found an old letter. It turned out the letter was from a Patricia Hall to her lover Robert Adams who happened to be a bank robber who stole fifty-thousand dollars from the Hastings National Bank. Fifty-thousand dollars I'm convinced is hidden somewhere in town. And I'm going to find it.

"The name is way too long. I thought you were going to come up with a new one," Aspen remarks.

I'll get right on it. As soon as I finish the fifty-thousand other things I have to do. I grit my teeth to stop myself from speaking. Complaining about the gazillion odd jobs I do to pay the rent will lead to questions I don't want to answer. Questions about what I'm doing with my life. I have a plan. Really, I do. It may not be going according to schedule, but it exists. Promise.

Lilac rolls her eyes. "I'm not interested in the name of this endeavor. I'm curious why we're having this meeting now. Have you uncovered new information?"

"I had an idea," I say, and everyone groans. "What's with the groans?"

"Every time you have an idea someone lands in jail," Juniper says.

I hold up a finger. "One time. One time you had to spend a whole five minutes in a jail cell. Will you get over it already?"

I don't mention the other times I've spent in jail. What they don't know won't hurt them. Besides, it doesn't count if the charges are dropped.

"Easy for you to say. You're the one who ended up on a date with Officer Peace while I ended up with stitches."

"I told you not to stand too close to the rocket."

"And I told you it was a bad idea, but did you listen? No. You never do."

Aspen claps her hands. "Ladies. Ladies. There's no sense going over old ground. I think Ashlyn has learned her lesson about rockets."

Lilac sighs. "I told you using a model rocket was a bad idea."

I giggle. "Because your idea of using a real rocket was better?"

"I've always wanted to build a rocket."

I cock an eyebrow. "Rocket doesn't exactly spell environmental engineer."

Lilac is an environmental engineer who works for the town. Since Winter Falls' claim to fame is being the first carbon neutral town in the world, she has a lot of work to do. She's currently tackling some biomass energy project. Don't ask me any questions, though. I never met a science class I liked.

"Which is why I didn't build one."

"Juniper!" Ellery screeches. "Your cat is doing the creepy stare thing. I swear he's plotting how to tear my face off with as much pain as possible."

Juniper grunts before standing and picking up the cat. She cuddles the animal to her chest before kissing its nose. "Meowise wouldn't hurt a fly," she proclaims before switching to baby talking her cat. "Would you, girl?"

I snort. "Sure she wouldn't because she's not the one who leaves little presents of dead mice and vole at the back door for me to find in the morning."

Juniper kisses the cat's nose. "It's her way of showing her affection."

Another reason I need my business to earn more money. I need to find my own place to live before I become the victim of the cat. I swear I've woken up with her staring down at my face, plotting my murder, on more than one occasion.

"Can we get on with this meeting? I'm meeting Lyric at *Electric Vibes* as soon as we're finished here," Aspen says.

Ellery rolls her eyes. "As if you didn't spend most of the day with your fiancé already."

"Watch it. Your jealousy is showing."

"I could do with a margarita," Juniper adds.

Aspen frowns. "You weren't invited."

"You're not the owner of *Electric Vibes*. If I want to go to the bar and drink a margarita, you can't stop me. Everyone knows I'm Lennon's favorite West sister."

Lennon is the owner of the bar. His favorite West sister is whichever West sister is picking up the bar tab.

"I could use a drink," Lilac adds, and everyone gapes at her. "What? I can have a bad day, too."

"What's wrong? Did one of your sexual partners stand you up?" Lilac announced last month at book club that she has several sexual partners with whom she has 'arrangements'. I'm still shocked, to be honest.

She purses her lips. "As a matter of fact, I had to cancel a meeting, because my boss asked me to work during lunchtime."

Aspen rubs her hands together. "Can you describe your grumpy boss to us? I need imagery."

Ellery smacks Aspen's shoulder. "What are you talking about? Why would you need imagery? You're the one having all the fiancé sex you can manage."

Aspen smirks. "It's true. I am."

The green monster in me roars to be let out to unleash its anger about how unfair the world is on Aspen. I shove the monster back down. It's wrong. Aspen spent a decade in misery because of a misunderstanding with Lyric. She doesn't deserve my anger.

"Now the dog's eyeballing me as if he's planning to rip my throat out," Ellery says.

Juniper sighs before grabbing the dog by its collar and pulling him away from her. "Bark Twain would never rip your throat out. Lick you to death? Yes. Hurt you? Never."

Bark Twain proceeds to prove her point by licking her face.

"Do you know how many bacteria and parasites are on a dog's tongue?" Lilac asks. When no one answers her, she lists them. "Salmonella, pasteurella, campylobacter, cryptosporidium, leptospira, giardia, ringworm, and hookworm."

"You don't have any silly bacteria or parasites. Do you Bark Twain?" Great. The baby talking to dogs portion of the evening has commenced. This could last a while.

Chapter 3

Down for the count – to be defeated by a stupid extension cord you didn't notice on the floor because someone thinks he's the boss of you

I wave to Petal, the owner of *Sensual Scents,* as I stroll down Main Street toward *The Inn on Main.*

"Ashlyn," she bellows to stop me.

There goes my plan of making my way down Main Street without interruption. I should know better.

I swallow my sigh and smile. "How are you, Petal?"

"I'm doing well. Ever since your sister recommended we use frosted glass instead of curtains, things in the bedroom have really heated up. Orion can really let loose when he doesn't have to worry about me setting fire to the place."

A picture of Petal and Orion having sexy times flashes into my mind, and I have to bite my tongue to stop from groaning. I'm far too visual a person. I have absolutely no problems with anyone having sex. Go for it is my motto in life. But I can't help visualizing the act itself, which tends to freak me out when the person talking is nearly as old as my grandmother.

"I bet the fire department appreciates your efforts."

In truth, the volunteer Fire Department in Winter Falls gets a kick out of being summoned for Petal's little candle mishaps. I know for a fact Lyric's brother, River, enjoys lecturing the sex candle shop owner about how dangerous candles can be.

"I need to get going. Have a nice day, Petal."

"Are you off to visit Rowan? That hunk can eat crackers in my bed any day."

"Don't make me tell Orion on you," I admonish her before hurrying away.

I am not on my way to visit Rowan by the way. It's not my fault I need to pass his bakery en route to *The Inn on Main*. But I will not glance in the window and torture myself with what I can't have. Not today at least. Just to be safe, I cross to the opposite side of the street from *Bake Me Happy*.

I wave at Aspen as I pass her bookstore. Next up is the diner. The owner, Gracious, rushes out. It's official. I should have stuck to the side streets.

"Ashlyn Dream West, you have a lot of explaining to do."

Great. What did I do now? I'm the first to admit I have a slight – very slight – tendency to get in trouble. It's not my fault. Trouble is attracted to me as if I'm one end of a great big magnet and it's the other end.

I widen my eyes and flutter my eyelashes. "I don't know what you're talking about."

She wags her finger at me. "Don't act all innocent, Missy. You haven't been innocent since the day you decided to give me a heart attack by planting a dead mouse in my purse."

"Irresponsible?" What is he talking about? I return my attention to the boxes. "Whatever. I'm none of your business. Move along now."

"Get off the ladder."

I keep my attention firmly planted on the boxes in front of me. "I'm not getting off the ladder."

"Your sister sent me up here to make sure you're safe. Now, get off the ladder."

I puff out a breath of air. Of course, he's here filling in as my non-existent big brother once again.

"I don't need anyone to check on me. I'm perfectly fine."

"You're going to fall and break your neck."

"I promise to be careful. There. Satisfied? You've done your big brother duty. You may leave now."

Hands grasp my calves. Big, strong hands. Ugh! I don't need to be thinking about how big and strong Rowan's hands are. And now I'm imagining how those big, strong hands would feel on the rest of my body. While I'm naked. Dammit.

"Get down from the ladder," Rowan orders from between clenched teeth.

Poof! There went my fantasy of him getting all handsy with naked Ashlyn.

"Fine!" I shriek. "I can come back later," I mumble under my breath.

He releases my calves to steady the ladder as I descend. When I reach the bottom, he doesn't move, and I end up cocooned by his body. I can feel the heat of his body emanating through his shirt. I feel safe and warm surrounded by him. Too bad he doesn't wrap his arms around me.

No, Ashlyn. We don't want his arms around us. We're getting over him, remember?

I shove at his chest. "Move, you big oaf."

He drops his hands and steps back. "Promise me you won't come back here and climb the ladder."

I cross my arms over my chest. "Why would I promise you anything?"

I'm a big fat fraud. I'd promise him the world for a simple kiss.

He grabs my hand. "Let's get out of here."

He drags me toward the door, but I wrench my hand from his. "I don't need an escort."

I'm too busy fuming at the hulk wannabe and forget to pay attention to where I'm walking. I trip on an extension cord and go flying. I land on my foot and hear a distinct snap as pain radiates throughout my foot and ankle before shooting up my leg.

"I think I broke my foot," I hiss before the pain becomes too much and it's lights out.

Chapter 4

Drop the ball – to act like a numbskull, therefore, causing an innocent person injury

ROWAN

I pace the waiting room of the hospital as I wait to hear how Ashlyn is doing. I clench my hands as I relive the moment her eyes closed, and she lost consciousness. I gathered her in my arms and ran as fast as I could to the police station where there's a vehicle available for any emergency a resident may have.

Normally, I love the Winter Falls' policy of no gas guzzling cars on its streets but now I'm worried the extra five minutes it took me to get Ashlyn to the hospital will prove disastrous.

"Why haven't we heard anything yet?" I ask the room again.

The waiting room is full of Ashlyn's family. Her parents and all four of her sisters sit quietly as they wait for news. How can they sit there all calm? Don't they realize what a big deal it is to lose consciousness? Ashlyn could have a concussion or some other traumatic brain injury.

Mrs. West stands and grasps my shoulders. She makes me feel like a giant since I'm easily a foot taller than her. She's just an itty-bitty thing. Unlike her daughter who gets her height from her dad.

Ashlyn is tall and thin, except for her ass. I want to sink my fingers into her round globes. And now I'm thinking about sex with the woman's daughter. I'm going to hell.

Mrs. West squeezes my shoulders. "She's going to be fine, Rowan. This isn't the first time she's broken a bone."

Ellery snorts. "Not even close. Remember the time she fell out of the tree and broke her arm?"

"Of course, I remember. She was spying on me and Lyric in the treehouse," Aspen says.

"At least, she won't cry all night long with a broken foot. Unlike when she fell into the poison ivy," Juniper comments.

Aspen sighs. "And that time she was spying on me and Lyric in the falls."

Lilac's brow wrinkles as she studies her older sister. "How did you manage to finish high school with all the fooling around you did?"

Aspen's cheeks darken while Ellery bursts into laughter. "Maybe because she set off the fire alarm every time there was a math test, she didn't study for."

Mrs. West slams her hands on her hips. "What? You mean to tell me I had the fire alarm company come to the school several times to check what was wrong with the fire alarm system when it was you this whole time?"

Mrs. West was the high school English teacher when I attended high school and now she's the principal of the school.

Relief hits me in the chest, and I have to steady myself with a hand against the wall. Ashlyn's okay. A broken ankle sucks, but it's not life threatening.

"Can we take her home now?" Mrs. West asks.

"Home?" I blurt out. "Shouldn't she be monitored if she's passing out from pain?"

"She's been given some pain medication," the doctor answers. "She's lucid and asking when she can escape this death trap. If there aren't any more questions?" He doesn't wait for a response before leaving.

"Okay," Mrs. West says. "I think Dad and I should bring her home with us."

"No way," Juniper responds. "She'll lose her mind if she has to stay with you two lovebirds."

Aspen clears her throat and indicates the hallway with a tilt of her head. What does she mean? I cock an eyebrow. She points to the hallway and mouths *go!*

While the West family argues about where to accommodate Ashlyn while she recovers, I sneak down the hall toward her room.

"Finally!" she yells when I walk in. Her brow wrinkles when she glances over and realizes it's me. "Sorry. I thought you were Juniper coming to break me out of here."

Despite being in a hospital and in pain, she's gorgeous. Her long, blonde hair is piled up on top of her head, but several strands have escaped and frame her face. Her bright blue eyes are dulled slightly with pain, but they continue to stare at me as if she can detect every secret I'm trying to hide from her. She's

Aspen's eyes widen as she gazes up at her mom. "You mean, you didn't know?"

"I assumed my daughter wouldn't commit a felony by setting off a false fire alarm."

Lilac clears her throat. "I don't think pulling a fire alarm is a felony."

Mrs. West's jaw clenches and I fear she's going to throw herself at her far too logical daughter. Before any blood can be shed, the doctor enters the room.

"West family?"

The family gathers around the doctor while I hang back. I'm not a member of their family. No matter how much I want to be. But it'll never happen. I don't deserve to have the love of a woman, especially not Ashlyn's.

"Ashlyn is doing well. She broke her ankle, but it was a simple break. There's no need for surgery. We've reset it and she'll be in a cast for six weeks. Otherwise, she's fine."

Before anyone else has a chance to speak, I do, "But why did she lose consciousness? Is she concussed?"

As a former football player, I'm very aware of how dangerous hits to the head can be. A concussion is more serious than people think.

The doctor peers up at me and his eyes widen. I'm used to the reaction. Being six-foot-five and having broad shoulders garners a lot of astonished looks.

"She didn't hit her head. She passed out from the pain."

usually smiling and laughing at the world, but now there are brackets around her mouth. She's in pain and I don't like it one bit.

"She's down the hall."

"Tell the truth. Is my mom with them?" At my nod, she sighs. "Mom is going to insist I stay with them."

"You're staying with me." The words coming out of my mouth shock me as much as they do Ashlyn.

Her nose scrunches. "I'm sorry. I think I'm hallucinating. These drugs they gave me must be better than I thought."

"Why do you think you're hallucinating?"

She snorts. "I couldn't have possibly heard the big, bad Rowan insist I stay at his house."

I cross my arms over my chest and watch with more than a bit of satisfaction as her eyes flare. "Why not?"

Her eyebrows fly up and her mouth drops open. "You're seriously asking me?" When I remain silent, she continues, "Um, maybe because you can barely stand the sight of me."

"What makes you say that?"

"It's this little thing most people refer to as 'the truth'."

"I don't hate you."

"Ya coulda fooled me."

Crap. I don't want her to hate me. I don't want to want her either, but my body yearns for hers. It has since she was sixteen. Since I was twenty-four at the time, I thought I was a sick fuck and avoided her for years. But I couldn't avoid her anymore when I moved back to town after my life fell apart.

"I get it," she says and draws me out of my fantasies of her.

"Get what?"

"This." She motions between the two of us. "You feel guilty about my broken ankle. You think it's your fault."

"It is my fault. I shouldn't have dragged you out of the attic the way I did."

She rolls her eyes. "Listen to me carefully. I'll speak slowly for you. This is not your fault."

A shiver travels down my spine at the sound of her voice. Ashlyn is a gorgeous woman, but her deep, raspy voice makes me want to throw her down and have my wicked way with her. I shove those thoughts out of my mind. Now is not the time. Never is the time. I don't deserve her.

I grunt. "Agree to disagree."

"Fine. Whatever. Can you send my family in? I'm ready to go home."

"I told you. You're not going home. You're staying with me until you can walk."

She grits her teeth. "No, I am not."

Her growling in her raspy voice is not helping matters.

The door flies open and Mrs. West rushes in. Behind her, Aspen mouths *sorry* to me. I give her a chin lift. I appreciate her allowing me some time alone with Ashlyn to apologize for getting her hurt.

"Awesome!" Ashlyn's hands fly into the air. "I'm busting out of this place. Whoo-hoo!"

The woman is crazy. She thinks breaking her ankle is some big adventure. I shouldn't be surprised. She seizes every day like life is an adventure and she's got the front seat on the roller coaster.

Lilac bumps into me. "You're still here?"

"I'm on my way." Because there's no way I can convince Ashlyn to come stay with me with her entire family in the room.

She sticks out her hand. "Thank you for getting my sister to the hospital as quickly as you did."

She has a firm grasp. "You're welcome."

I try to extract my hand, but she uses her grip to pull me close and whispers, "Don't worry. We've got your back." She releases my hand and winks.

I back away from her. I don't know what she's talking about and, frankly, I'm a bit scared to find out.

"Um, thanks?" I mutter before making my escape.

I'll figure some other way to make it up to Ashlyn for causing her to break her ankle and being laid up for six weeks. Laid up? Shit. Ashlyn can't do her plethora of odd jobs if she's laid up. How is she going to afford rent? The situation is worse than I thought. I'll figure out a way to help, though. I have to. This is all my fault. More proof I don't deserve love.

Chapter 5

End Around – evasive maneuvering causing one person to get what he wants while another person feels railroaded

I sigh as I collapse onto the sofa. I lift my foot to rest it on the coffee table, but it lands harder than I intended, and I end up whimpering when an unexpected flash of pain shoots up my leg. I close my eyes and let my head fall against the back of the sofa.

"I think I'll sleep here," I mumble to no one in particular.

Bark Twain jumps onto the sofa next to me and sticks his big chin on my thigh. I scratch behind his ears and his tail thumps. Meowise is not happy with my attention being on her nemesis, the dog, and meows while clawing at my cast while Dale the chipmunk climbs onto my shoulder.

Indiana Bones refuses to be left out of the fun and nudges his way between me and the side of the sofa. He doesn't care if there's enough room for his furry butt or not. He nudges and nudges until I'm forced to scoot over for him.

I open my eyes to find my family staring at me, their gazes full of amusement. "Don't say a word."

"One step at a time," I answer as if it's the most obvious thing in the world.

"Your father and I decided," she begins.

Dad lifts his hands and steps back. "Leave me out of this. I want my baby to be comfortable. If she's comfortable staying here and sleeping in her own bed, I think she should stay here."

Mom turns on him. "What part of 'leave me out of this' do you not understand? You can't say leave me out of this and give an opinion afterwards. It's not how things work."

"Mom. Dad," I holler but they ignore me to continue bickering.

"Well, I'm definitely not going home with them. They have loud make-up sex after every argument."

Dad's eyes light up and he steps closer to Mom. Great. Now I'm imagining them getting busy. I don't need to use my imagination much as I've barged in on them too many times to count.

"Don't be such a prude, babycakes," Aspen says and I, being the mature adult I'm trying to convince everyone I am, stick my tongue out at her.

The door bangs open, and I glance over to find the object of my every desire standing there. What's he doing here? He knows where I live? How does he know where I live?

"You're staying with me," Rowan grumbles, and I shiver as his grumpy voice hits me in all the best spots.

"No, I am not." Huh. Would you listen to me? My voice didn't tremble once. *Go, Ashlyn!*

"Put her in a skirt and bowler hat and she's the spitting im of Mary Poppins," Ellery says.

"Did you keep her costume from the time she played Mary Poppins in the high school play? I can run home and get it," Aspen adds.

"Ha! Ha! Very funny." I scratch my nose with my middle finger.

"No one is going anywhere," Mom declares before glaring at me. "And don't think I didn't see you, young lady."

Juniper bounds down the stairs and drops a bag on the floor near the door. "Here you go."

"What are you doing with my bag?"

She rolls her eyes. "Duh. I packed your things."

"Packed my things? We agreed in the hospital I'd stay here at home with you in this apartment while I convalesce."

"I don't think you should stay here with all of Juniper's animals—"

"Hey," Juniper cries and cuts Mom off. "There's nothing wrong with my animals. Look for yourself." She motions to me. "They're comforting her."

Indiana Bones chooses the moment to let out a loud fart. I cover my face while trying not to gag at the foul smell. Meanwhile, Meowise's attempts to claw my cast off increase until her claws are digging into my leg. Ouch. Such comfort these animals offer.

"Besides," Mom ignores Juniper to continue, "how are you going to maneuver the stairs with your cast and crutches?"

"Ash, you can't be climbing up and down those stairs all damn day." He points out.

I roll my eyes. "I won't be. I'll climb down them once in the morning and climb up them once in the evening. There's a half bath on this level and a full bathroom on the second floor, so there's no need to be climbing up and down all day."

"And what about your work?"

My work is completely unaffected by a broken ankle. Oh wait. He's not talking about my business. No one except Juniper knows about my secret business. He's referring to my odd jobs. Those I won't be doing for a while.

"Obviously, I can't be running around doing all kinds of odd jobs while my foot is in this cast. Once I get a walking cast put on in a few weeks, I'll be back in business."

"No, you won't. You need to rest up until your ankle is properly healed."

"Dude, it's called a walking cast for a reason. You should know this. You were a professional athlete. Injuries happen."

"And they need time to heal."

I ignore his comment to go on the attack. "Why are you here? You're not my keeper."

"Someone has to be."

His words slice through me. Once again, he's reminding me of how I'm nothing to him but a little sister he has to watch out for. Ouch.

I sweep my arm through the room. "I have my family to help me out. I don't need you."

Aspen raises her hand. "Not it." I glare at her. "What? If you think Mom and Dad have a lot of sex—"

I throw my hand up in a stop sign. "Enough."

"Not it as well," Lilac says.

"Really?"

She shrugs. "I live in a one-bedroom apartment on the second floor."

Dang. She's got me there.

When I glance Ellery's way, she holds up her hands. "Nope. I live in the carriage house behind the inn. It's also a one-bedroom."

"I guess I'm staying here."

"Or," Rowan growls, "you can get your head out of your ass and admit you need my help. I have a three-bedroom ranch house."

As if I don't know what type of house he has. And I certainly haven't drooled over the adorable white with gray trim house more times than I can count. Nor have I happened to jog past it on my way out to River's goat farm a time or two. A fifteen-minute detour on a five-minute commute is totally normal, right?

But nobody – and I do mean nobody – tells me to get my head out of my ass.

"What is your problem? You can't possibly want me staying with you for several weeks."

He grunts, and it's not hard to figure out what he's thinking.

"There's no reason to feel guilty. It's a broken ankle. It will heal."

"It's my fault it's broken, and you can't do your work anymore. It will make me feel better if you let me help you out."

I snort. Make him feel better? I wasn't put on this earth to make him feel better. Except my heart – the stupid organ – beats faster at the idea of being able to do something to make the big, strong Rowan feel better.

"You don't have to worry about being around me."

Ha! Me worried about being around him? Not hardly. No, I'm worried I'll get entirely too used to being around him and my heart will break into a million tiny pieces when I move back home, and he goes back to pretending I don't exist in between bouts of pretending to be my big brother.

"I'm barely home since I have to be at the bakery by 4 a.m. six days a week and we're open until four in the afternoon."

"Just stay with him. You know you want to," Aspen goads.

I narrow my eyes at her, and she smirks. I don't know what she thinks she's doing. My sisters – okay fine probably every resident in the entire town – know I've crushed on Rowan since I was sixteen. They also know Rowan's not interested in me. Do they think us being in close proximity is going to change his mind?

It won't. If stopping by his bakery every dang day for a year hasn't changed his mind yet, nothing will. I rub a hand over my chest when it starts to ache.

"Fine."

The word is barely out of my mouth before Rowan's stomping across the living room and picking me up. I slap his chest.

Ugh. Bad idea. Now I know how hard and strong his chest muscles feel. This is the worst idea ever.

"What are you doing?" I manage to sound indignant and not all breathy. Go me!

"I'm carrying you to my golf cart."

"I can walk. I have two perfectly good legs."

He cocks an eyebrow at me.

"Amendment. One perfectly good leg and a pair of crutches."

"I'm not making you hobble around on those crutches a few hours after you passed out from the pain."

Geez. I am never going to hear the end of it for passing out.

"Here we go." He sets me on the back of the golf cart, making certain my leg is elevated, before returning to the house to grab my bag and crutches.

I glance over my shoulder and notice my entire family is standing at the front window watching the interaction. They're enjoying the situation entirely too much. I avert my gaze before the temptation to flip them off becomes too much. As Mom has reminded me on too many occasions to count, she's not too old to ground me.

"Gee, Ash. What do you have in this bag? It's heavy as hell."

I'm not answering his question. I assume Juniper – aka the sister secret keeper – packed my necessities. I hope I can find a quiet place to do my work at Rowan's house because I'll be relying on the income from my business for the next month or two.

"Hold on tight," Rowan orders as he switches on the golf cart.

Nope. No more holding on tight. I've been holding on to the sexy former football player entirely too tightly for too long. But how am I going to let go when I'm living in his house? I wish I could order a container to encase my heart in for its protection because I'm going to need it.

Chapter 6

Get the ball rolling – to begin an endeavor whether or not the players know the endeavor is beginning

ROWAN

I drive slowly back to my house. I've got precious cargo on the back of my golf cart. I'm not going to cause her any more pain than I already have.

"Geez. At this rate, I could have crutched here faster," Ashlyn complains.

I grunt because all I seem to be able to do when Ashlyn's around is become a grump or grunt at her. Every time I try to engage her in conversation, I end up telling her what to do. To the point, she thinks I fancy myself her big brother.

My feelings for Ashlyn are not what a big brother should feel for his sister. Not even close. Whenever I see the blonde beauty with her big smile on her face, I want to pull her near and kiss the smile clean off her face until she's moaning and begging me to touch every single inch of her body.

And now I'm aroused while the woman of my fantasies sits less than a foot away from me completely oblivious as to how I feel. Unfortunately, she needs to remain oblivious, because

I am never acting on those fantasies. Not when I can't make a woman happy. And Ashlyn deserves all the happiness in the world.

"Stop complaining, brat."

"I'm not a brat," she grumbles.

Crap. There I go again making her feel like shit. More proof of why I can't have a woman.

"Here we are," I say when I pull to a stop in front of my house.

I stare up at my home and wonder what Ash thinks of it. Does she love ranch houses, or does she prefer big colonial houses similar to the one she grew up in?

While I'm contemplating houses, Ash wobbles past me.

"What the hell?" I bark and jump out of the golf cart. "What are you doing?"

She rolls her eyes. "What does it look like I'm doing?"

Her words are indignant but she's struggling for breath. I step toward her to pick her up and carry her inside, but she leans away from me.

"Stop! I won't have you carrying me around."

I fist my hands to stop myself from reaching for her. When I carried her before, it felt right having her in my arms as if she was always meant to be there. But she's correct. I shouldn't be hauling her around. I can't get used to holding her when I know I can't keep her.

"Let me get the door for you."

I hurry past her to open the door. It's not locked. No one locks their door in Winter Falls except for during tourist season.

Since October has arrived and tourist season is over, the door's unlocked.

I crush the door handle in my hand as I watch Ash navigate the two steps to my porch. I forgot about those damn steps. I should have carried her. It's as if she can read my mind.

"Shut it," she growls. "I can handle two freaking steps."

I know she can. This woman can handle whatever life throws at her. Bullies, a goat determined to hump her leg, my grumpy ass. She can handle all of it with a smile on her face. But I don't want her to have to. I want to carry all her burdens for her. I do some deep breathing exercises in an effort to force those thoughts out of my mind. I can't have her, no matter how much I might want to.

I motion inside my house. "Get your ass moving."

Her shoulder brushes against my chest as she passes me, and my body tightens and heats from the minuscule contact. I can't wait to experience how my body will respond to more contact. No. I clear my throat. I can't. Because Ash and I together is never happening. No matter how much my body yearns to throw her down on the floor and have my way with her.

"Which way is my room?" she asks, and the spell her body has woven over me is broken.

"Food first."

"What are you? A caveman? Food first. Grunt. Me big man. Grunt. Me make all the rules. Grunt." She giggles at her own joke and light and goodness pours out of her. I want to bathe in her light, but I know I'd extinguish her light if I got too close.

"You need to eat. Pain meds without food is a surefire way to upset your stomach."

"You would know," she teases in a sing-song voice, but her eyes widen when she realizes what she said, and she slams a hand over her mouth.

I wave away her concern. Yes, it's true, I blew out my knee playing football and the injury ruined my career, but I'm not going to break down and cry each and every time someone alludes to it. I'm a big boy. I've made peace with my past.

"Come on. I'll make you something to eat. Pasta okay?"

"You can cook?"

"Did you forget I own a bakery?"

Bake Me Happy is my pride and joy. Maybe it's weird for a six-foot-five former football player to own a bakery, but I don't care. I've loved baking since my mother sat me on the kitchen counter and taught me the difference between salted and unsalted butter. Plus, there's the challenge of creating baked goods made with local, organically grown ingredients. I always did love a challenge.

"Baking and cooking are not the same thing."

She isn't wrong. "Yes, I can cook," I tell her.

I walk to the kitchen to get started on dinner. The living/kitchen/dining areas are open concept so she can see into the kitchen from where she's standing. It's a massive space. Since I'm a big guy, I need to have room to move around. I also test out new recipes at home making having a big kitchen with multiple ovens a necessity.

"Get comfortable while I make us some dinner."

She doesn't listen to me. Of course not. I don't know why I'd expect her to at this point. I can tell by the brackets around her mouth she's in pain and needs to rest, but if I mention her pain, she'll never rest. I grit my teeth before I say something I shouldn't.

I decide on a simple pasta as it's the quickest dish I can put together. While I throw together a Bolognese sauce, Ash explores my house. There's not a whole lot to explore as I prefer to keep things neat and tidy.

The living room is dominated by a U-shaped sofa. In front of the sofa is my pride and joy – an eighty-five-inch television.

"Holy shrine to the football gods, you could host Sunday football with this setup," Ash yells.

"Do you like football?"

In my experience, they are two types of women who claim to like football – those who love the game and those who are trying to impress a man. I doubt Ash would ever try to impress a man. No, if the man isn't impressed with her how she is, she's not interested.

She rolls her eyes at me. "Am I a red-blooded American? Of course, I love football."

"Real football?" I press. "And not some fantasy league?"

"Watch it, oaf. I kick ass in fantasy league football."

My hands stop chopping onion long enough to glance over at her. "Want to put your money where your mouth is?"

Her nose wrinkles and she bites her lip and I wonder what possessed me to use the word mouth in relation to Ash. Now, I'm imagining those luscious lips biting me instead of her lip.

Blood rushes south to my groin and I have to lock my jaw before a moan slips out.

"You're in trouble now, oaf. I'll accept your wager, but I don't want money."

Is it too much to ask for her to want sexual favors if she wins? Damnit. No. I will not be indulging in sexual favors with this woman no matter how much I may want to.

"What do you want?" I manage to force the question out of my mouth.

"A year's supply of peanut butter cookies."

I tap my chin and pretend to consider it. "And what do I get when I win?"

She snorts. "When? You won't win, but if you do…" she pauses and I grip the knife in my hand tight before I do something incredibly stupid such as haul her into my arms, "…you can have whatever you want."

Wrong thing to say, Ash. Wrong thing to say. Because what I want, she can't handle.

"I'll think about it and let you know." I force myself to return to chopping the onion. "Get comfortable on the sofa. I'll bring the food out when it's ready."

I expect her to bitch at me for ordering her around, but she must be in more pain than I thought, because she plops down on the sofa and grabs the remote control to switch on the television.

"I'm stealing this television when I leave."

"You do not mess with a man's television," I grumble at her.

She giggles and settles in to watch a basketball game.

I hurry to finish the pasta before she falls asleep. I wasn't joking earlier. It's important to eat with pain medication or you'll end up with stomach distress. I learned that lesson the hard way.

When I bring her the plate of food I've prepared, her eyes bug out of her head as she assesses the pasta. "Holy fresh guacamole! Exactly how much food do you think I eat in a day? I know my ass is big, but it's not *that* big."

Her ass is fucking perfect. It's the perfect size for my hands. And there goes all the blood rushing from my head down to my groin again.

"Here," I grumble and practically drop the plate in her lap.

"Fine, but I will have desert regardless of whether I finish all of this."

Let's see if she can eat the pasta without falling asleep with her face in the plate first.

"I think I can allow one cookie," I tell her instead of mentioning how tired she appears. I'm not a complete idiot after all.

She scarfs down half of the plate before setting it on the coffee table and settling into the sofa. By the time I finish my meal, she's fast asleep. I clean up the dishes before carrying her to my suite. It's the only bedroom with an attached bathroom and I don't want her walking far to use the facilities. Or at least that's the reason I'm telling myself for why I want her in my bed.

After I settle her, my gaze lingers on the woman of my dreams laying there in my bed. She reminds me of an angel with her blonde hair spread out around the pillow. Bringing her here was a mistake but I'll be damned if I regret it for one moment.

Chapter 7

To come out of left field – when Mr. Overprotector is in on the surprise

"You're not going."

"You're not going," I mimic like I'm a teenager being put on house arrest by her mom instead of a full-fledged adult being held captive by a burly man.

Great. Now, I can't stop imagining Rowan in a pirate's outfit. I nearly fan myself when I think of his massive chest being exposed by the pirate shirt. Does he have hair on his chest? Can I curl my fingers into it? Or is his chest smooth and hairless and I can glide my hands over it without disruption? Inquiring minds want to know.

"You broke your ankle last week. You should keep your leg elevated, not go bar hopping." Grumpy dude had to open his mouth and ruin my pirate fantasy, didn't he?

I lean forward as far as I can without tipping forward on these dang crutches and get right up in his face. "I'm not going bar hopping. I'm going to *Electric Vibes* for the monthly pub quiz. I can't miss a pub quiz. My team relies on me for the sports questions. Ellery, Aspen, Lilac, and Juniper are useless when it comes to sports."

He crosses his arms over his chest and his biceps flex with the movement. My eyes are drawn there, and I can't help but wonder if I can wrap my hand around his bicep or if his bicep is wider than my hand.

"Alcohol and pain meds do not mix."

"Good thing I didn't take any pain meds today then, isn't it?" I fire back at him.

He growls. "You didn't take any pain meds?" He prowls down the hallway toward the bedrooms. "Where do you keep them? In the bathroom?"

I use my crutch to slap his calf. "Stop! I don't need any pain medication. It's a broken ankle. The only reason I have the pain meds in the first place is because of the whole being a complete wimp and passing out thing."

My face heats at the memory. Why, oh why, am I the one person in the world who passes out because of a broken bone? Ugh. So embarrassing.

Rowan actually stops his prowl down the hallway. "You're positive you don't need something to help with the pain? I have some aspirin."

I roll my eyes. "Dude, if I want aspirin, I have some. I'm a woman. I have a complete pharmacy in my make-up bag."

He blows out a breath of air, and I realize I've won this round. "But you're still not going to the pub."

I guess I haven't won this round after all. "I'm going. I'll message Lyric. My future brother-in-law is the Chief of Police. He won't let you hold me captive."

I hope. You never know what the people of Winter Falls will do in any given situation. My sister Aspen appears determined to force Rowan and me together, and I fear she's roped her fiancé, the Chief of Police, into assisting her. Why do happily engaged people think it's okay to matchmake other people?

"Go ahead," he says and offers me his phone.

Well, shit. Lyric is definitely compromised. But none of this makes any sense.

Today's my birthday. I planned to meet up with my sisters at the bar to celebrate. Technically, my birthday celebration is Sunday at our weekly family dinner, but I can't let the actual day of my birthday slide by without some kind of celebration. It would be the height of depressing!

I bite my lip as I stare up at Rowan. He doesn't know it's my birthday either. I know everything about this man – his birthday, the day he was drafted into the NFL, the day he got married, the day he blew out his knee and his career ended, the day he got divorced – and he doesn't even know when my birthday is. If there ever was a big flashing red sign telling me this man is not for me, this would probably be it.

His phone beeps and he reads the message. "Get your shit. I'll drive you to the bar."

Wait! What? "Why did you change your mind?" I wave my hands in the air as if to erase my question and nearly end up nosediving to the floor. "Never mind. I'm ready. Let's go."

"Don't you need to spend an hour in the bathroom doing your make-up?"

I glare up at him. "Are you saying I'm ugly?"

He rubs his neck. "No?"

"Whatever. Let's go."

He bends down to lift me, and I swat him away. "I can walk, dude. In fact, I'll race your fat ass to the golf cart," I taunt before taking off.

I'm not blowing smoke. I am pretty fast on my crutches. It helps that my upper body is strong from all the helping out at Phoenix's farm I've done.

"Who's the fat ass now?" Rowan asks as he leans against the golf cart before I can make it there.

"Yeah, yeah," I mumble as I make my way to the rear of the cart. "The whole world knows about my fat ass. No need to rub it in."

His hands fist as he backpedals. "I wasn't. I didn't mean..."

I ignore the pain in my chest at the reminder of how my body is not attractive to him. It's not anything I didn't already know. I gesture in the general direction of *Electric Vibes.*

"To the bar, Jeeves."

Rowan sighs, but he doesn't bring up my unattractive behind again. Good thing, too, since I can feel my eyes itch. Wouldn't that be the height of embarrassment? Crying in front of my crush who thinks I'm a little girl who needs to be taken care of.

When we arrive at the bar, there's no music pouring out of the building and the lights are dim. I scan the area in confusion.

It's Saturday night *and* quiz night. This place should be hopping about now.

I allow Rowan to help me off the golf cart and follow him to the door.

"I know you don't want to stay. You go ahead home now. One of my sisters will bring me back later. Don't wait up for me." I give him a saucy wink.

He ignores me to open the door. "After you."

I enter the quiet bar and come to a screeching halt when I realize it's pitch black inside. What the heck is going on here? I feel Rowan place a hand on my lower back. His hand is big and strong, and I want to lean into it, but why is he touching me?

"Surprise!"

The lights flash on and people pop up from their hiding spots.

"Happy birthday!"

Rowan leans down to whisper in my ear, "Happy birthday, Ash."

I shiver and goosebumps break out on my skin from the feel of his breath against my skin. I lock my muscles to stop myself from arching my neck to give him better access. He doesn't want better access.

"I'm sorry I fought with you about coming," he says in a voice loud enough for everyone to hear. "They weren't finished with the decorations and asked me to stall you."

Before I have a chance to thank him for bringing me, my sisters attack.

"Happy birthday, babycakes!" They shout in unison before dragging me toward a chair in the middle of the room. It's decorated with streamers and paper flowers. We don't do balloons in Winter Falls. Even those ecologically friendly ones are banned.

Juniper props my foot up on a stool, and Aspen places a crown made of fabric flowers on my head. "For the birthday girl. You only turn twenty-four once in your life after all. Twenty-four and all grown up."

"Why do you keep emphasizing her age?" Lilac asks. "Everyone knows how old she is. We grew up in the same house as her after all."

Aspen elbows her and nods toward Rowan who I'm surprised to find hasn't left the bar. I figured he'd return home as soon as he dropped me. He's not much of a bar person. Of course, I can't fault him for it since he usually has to get up two hours after the bar closes to start baking delicious treats.

"Rowan knows how old she is," Lilac explains to Aspen. "He grew up here, too."

Juniper sighs before explaining to our relationship-studded sister, "She's trying to matchmake Rowan and Ashlyn."

Lilac's mouth purses as she considers the situation. "Is it too late to place my wager?"

"Yes!" I yell at the same moment Ellery yells no. I glare at her. "No betting on my relationship status."

Aspen leans close to hiss in my ear. "Not as much fun when you're the target, is it? Told you payback is a bitch."

I thought she'd pay me back for pushing her and Lyric back together by pranking me. Maybe placing some mayonnaise in my frosting jar. Not by matchmaking me with the one man in Winter Falls who I desire with all of my being but can never have.

"You're cruel."

"And you're narrow sighted."

"Whatever. Where are my presents?"

Lennon, the owner of *Electric Vibes,* arrives with a round of tequila shots. "There will be no presents until after the quiz."

I shrug. "As long as there are margaritas, I don't mind."

I lift my glass. "To me. On my birthday!"

"I don't think you can toast yourself. It's against etiquette rules," Lilac claims.

"And I don't care, Ms. Manners."

Lennon steps on stage and grasps the microphone. He smirks at me before speaking. "The theme of tonight's quiz will be … Ashlyn Dream West."

I groan. Talk about embarrassing. But I don't shy away from a challenge. Not even if the result is the revelation of all of my deep, dark secrets. I scan the room and notice Rowan hasn't left yet. He lifts an eyebrow in challenge. Game on, Rowan. Game on.

"I'm going to need a pitcher of margaritas stat, Lennon," I order in response and a cheer rises up from the crowd.

Chapter 8

Throw a curveball – when your temporary houseguest surprises you in such a way you nearly lose your mind

ROWAN

I put the finishing touches on the breakfast tray before carrying it toward my bedroom where Ashlyn is currently sleeping off her hangover. I'm surprised I managed to get her home without her falling out of the golf cart last night. She swayed and sang the theme song to *Gilligan's Island* the entire drive while I clung to her shirt in a desperate attempt to keep her butt planted in her seat. It worked. Barely. But it worked.

I toe the bedroom door open with my foot to discover the room's empty. The covers on the bed are ruffled from where Ash slept, but there's no sign of the woman herself. She must be in the bathroom. I set the tray on the bedside table before going in search of my errant guest. I stride toward the bathroom but halt when I hear voices coming from my walk-in closet.

"Ricardo, we can't. I'm to be married in the morning." Ash moans and my cock twitches while anger simultaneously blasts through my body. Who the hell is Ricardo?

"Oh god, but I want to. I really, really want to." Another moan has me seeing red. I march toward the door but pause with my hand on the handle when another voice speaks.

"My darling, we can. No one has to know."

"But won't he…" She gasps. "Please, do that again. Don't make me beg."

"What, my love? This?"

"Don't stop. Don't ever stop." Those words spoken in her deep, raspy voice has all the blood in my body rushing toward my groin.

"My darling, I wouldn't dare." The heat in my veins turns to ice at the man's response.

What the hell? Does she have a man in my closet with her? She brought a man to my house. To my bedroom. To my closet. I'm going to kill him.

I wrench the door open and stomp into the room. I freeze at the vision in front of me. Ash is sitting on the floor, leaning against the wall, with her foot propped up on a pillow. She's wearing headphones and speaking into a microphone. I scan the area, but she's definitely alone.

What's going on here? Is she having phone sex? Is she some sort of online call girl? There's one way to find out.

"What the hell are you doing?" I yell.

Ash startles and her computer slides from her lap onto the floor. She peers up at me with wide eyes. When she realizes who I am, her eyes narrow and she glares at me.

"What the hell, Rowan? Now, I'm going to have to record the entire session again." She groans and rubs her temples.

"Session? What are you talking about?"

"I'm narrating an audiobook. What did you think I was doing?"

I shrug.

"Crap on a cracker! You thought I was in here having phone sex?" she shrieks.

It sounds really bad when she says it. "No?"

"No?" She snorts. "What else could it be? You think I'm some kind of online prostitute?"

I whistle and glance away.

"You think I'm a prostitute?" she screams and tries to stand. I hurry to help her, but she shoves me away. "I don't need help from someone who thinks I'm a prostitute."

"I don't think you're a prostitute," I manage to say between grit teeth as I watch her struggle to stand. I reach out to help her again, but she bats my hands away.

"I saw your face. On a side note, never play poker with the old guard. Your poker face is non-existent. They'd steal your money and laugh all the way to the bank."

"Give me a break. I was shocked, okay? I came in here to treat you to breakfast in bed for your birthday and I hear sex sounds and a male voice coming from my closet. I'm allowed to be a bit confused."

She freezes. "Did you say breakfast in bed?"

I've got her now. Ash has the biggest sweet tooth of anyone I know, and I'm a baker.

"Yes." I indicate the bedside table where the tray sits.

"What did you make?"

"You'll have to see for yourself."

She bites her lip as she considers the tray.

"There might be pancakes," I tease.

"What kind of pancakes?"

I stuff my hands in my pockets and rock back on my heels. "Red velvet with cream cheese glaze."

She gasps and elbows her way past me into the bedroom. She throws her crutches on the ground and flops down on the bed.

"Feed me, Jeeves."

I chuckle as I place the tray on her lap. "I'll go grab the coffee."

"No coffee. I have to finish this recording today. Coffee wreaks havoc on my voice. I'd prefer herbal tea if you have some."

I don't have any herbal tea, but I'll buy all the herbal tea I can find in the store as soon as I can. I want Ash to feel welcome here. I want her to feel at home here. Shit. This can't be her home. Stop dreaming about stuff you can never have.

"Pineapple juice or apple juice will work as well."

"I have apple juice," I announce before scrambling out of the room to get her a glass.

When I return to the room with the juice, I find Ash moaning once again. This time it's over my pancakes. I enjoy how she digs into and loves food. I know she thinks her ass is too big from eating too much, but she's wrong. It's the perfect size.

"These pancakes are to die for," she mumbles around a bite. "Do you want a taste?"

She offers me a bite from her fork. I'm tempted just for the chance to be near her, but I shake my head instead. I need to stop fantasizing about the woman I can never have.

I drag a chair from the alcove in front of the window toward the bed. "Now, tell me. What's this whole recording thing about?"

She considers me as she finishes her pancakes. Only when her pancakes are eaten does she set her fork down before finally answering my question, "I narrate audiobooks."

"That was some steamy audiobook."

Her cheeks darken and she wiggles in the bed. "It's erotica," she mumbles.

"Say what?"

She blows out a puff of air. "It's erotica," she says louder this time.

"Erotica? As in romance novels?"

"Not necessarily. You have erotica and then you have erotic romance."

I'm an idiot. Why did I ask her to explain erotica to me? My cock, which has barely calmed down from listening to her raspy voice pretending to be in the throes of sex in the closet, perks up. It wants to listen to Ash narrate naughty scenes all day long before staging our own naughty scene.

I clear my throat. "And you make money doing this?"

"I do. Not as much as I want since my name isn't well-known yet, but I'm getting there. I have a few steady gigs from writers who release a book a month, but it's not enough to pay all my bills. I need more clients."

A light bulb goes off above my head as the past year finally makes sense. "This is why you do a million odd jobs. It isn't because you don't know what you want to do with your life. It's because you're still establishing yourself in your chosen career."

"Exactly," she says before sipping on her apple juice.

"And once you're established, you'll quit all those jobs and concentrate on this alone?" I push because I hate the idea of how hard she works. She works even harder than I thought since she must narrate these books at odd hours of the night.

"That's the plan."

There's one thing I don't understand. Why has she kept this a secret? And I know it must be a secret because if anyone else in town knew about it, everyone in town would know. Discretion is not a virtue in Winter Falls, but nosiness is.

"You haven't told anyone about this career path, have you?"

"Yes, I have. Juniper knows. Why do you think she packed my computer and my microphone and all my other gear?"

"But no one else knows." It's a statement, not a question. There's no way anyone else knows or I'd have heard about this business by now.

She shrugs and averts her gaze.

"Why haven't you told anyone?" I rear back when an idea hits me. "You're not embarrassed, are you? You do remember you live in Winter Falls."

I can't imagine why she'd be embarrassed. No one in this town shies away from discussing sex. Hell, her mom shoved a condom in my back packet when I was carrying Ash out of her home the day she broke her ankle. A condom I gave away to keep temptation at bay. Although, when it comes to Ash, temptation is never far away.

She sticks her tongue out at me. "Of course, I'm not embarrassed. I love what I do and I'm good at it, too. I want my business to make a decent wage before I tell everyone is all."

She's lying or at least not telling the whole truth. I don't know why. Ash isn't the type of woman to lie or shy away from the truth. Something's going on inside her head and I want to know what, but when I study her, I notice she's fiddling with the napkin on her breakfast tray.

I decide to let her off the hook. I don't want her to feel uncomfortable in my home. Besides, all this talk of her narrating erotica is not good for my blood circulation.

"Let's talk about a more important topic." Her eyebrow wings up in question. "How do you not have a hangover this morning? I saw how many tequila shots you drank last night."

Her body relaxes, and I realize I made the right choice. She deserves to be comfortable in her own home. Despite how temporary the situation is. And no matter how much I might wish it could be otherwise.

Chapter 9

Long shot – An attempt to solve a mystery despite the low chance of success

"I'M HERE, I'M HERE," Juniper announces as she darts inside of the storeroom at Aspen's bookstore.

"The question is why we're here," Lilac says.

Juniper shrugs. "I assumed Aspen wanted to tell us she's pregnant without any prying eyes around."

"What?" Ellery squeals. "You're pregnant?"

Aspen's eyes widen to the size of saucers. "I'm not pregnant. Why would you think I'm pregnant?"

"Why else are we having a secret meeting in the storeroom?" Juniper asks.

Aspen smiles at me. "Because someone finally did the deed with her crush."

"Yes!" Juniper jumps up and down. "I'm so happy for you," she tells me before sticking her hand out to Ellery. "Pay up."

Ellery scowls as she removes a five-dollar bill from her back pocket. I slap the money out of her hand.

"No one is paying up. Nothing happened."

Lilac's nose scrunches as she studies me. "Nothing happened? Rowan carried you out of the bar when you were drunk like you were his most prized possession—"

"And he has a super bowl ring," Aspen interrupts to say.

Lilac clears her throat. "As I was saying, he carried you out of the bar like you were his most prized possession and nothing happened?"

"Oh, come on. Didn't he help you to bed and then you accidentally pulled him into bed with you and your lips accidentally found his and voila commencement of sexy times?" Juniper waggles her eyebrows.

"That's a whole lot of accidentally going on. You sound experienced in this accidental commencement of sexy times endeavor," I say instead of admitting how I tried all of the above and got shot down by Rowan.

She shrugs. "What can I say? Accidents happen."

Aspen bumps my shoulder. "Yeah, Ashlyn. Accidents happen. Did his penis happen to accidentally find its way inside you?"

"No. And what a non-sexy way to describe sex." Trust me. As an erotic romance narrator, I'm an expert on ways to describe sex. "How many ways can I explain this to you? Nothing happened. He didn't even make a move when he brought me breakfast in bed."

"He made you breakfast in bed?" Juniper doesn't wait for me to respond before she turns to Ellery. "New bet."

I clap my hands to get everyone's attention. "We're not here to discuss my love life."

"Of course not." Lilac snorts. "It seems to be non-existent. You can hardly discuss a topic, which is non-existent."

I frown at her. "Gee, thanks, Lilac Bean."

"Why are you bringing out the middle name? I was merely stating the truth."

Sigh. Lilac doesn't mean to be hurtful, but her emotions don't work the same way as other people. She's not cold and unfeeling as some residents of Winter Falls would have you believe. She shows her emotions in different ways than most people is all. It can be abrasive, though, when she doesn't understand what you're going through.

Juniper huffs and crosses her arms over her chest as she taps her toe in impatience. "If we're not here to re-hash every single second of a sexual encounter between Rowan and Ashlyn, and we're not here to congratulate Aspen because she's pregnant, what the hell are we here for?"

I'm not personally offended by Ms. Grumpy's words. I know any time I force her away from her precious animals at the Wildlife Refuge, there's a ninety-nine percent chance she'll be annoyed. I feel sorry for any man who tries to capture her attention since she loves animals more than humans, including me and the rest of the family.

"It's time to continue our adventure with The Mystery of the Black Hat Bandit's Missing Loot," I announce with a whoop.

"Yeah!" Aspen claps. "What did you find out? And don't think I'm not still annoyed with you for going to the inn to search for clues without me."

I glare at her. I tried to include her in the search, but she was too busy trying to set me up with Rowan to listen to my ideas.

"If you two are done glaring at each other, can we begin? I need to get back to the inn."

Ellery always needs to get back to the inn. She works entirely too hard as evidenced by the dark smudges under her eyes. Her face is pale now, too. I hope my not being able to help out with the cleaning hasn't caused her to work even harder than she usually does.

I'd offer to help her out, but Rowan would lose his mind if he found out I'm cleaning. I'm barely allowed to stumble to the bathroom on my own when he's around. The man takes his big brother duties way too seriously.

"I read Old Man Mercury's book," I begin.

"I don't think we should refer to him as Old Man Mercury anymore," Aspen interrupts to say. "It sounds derogatory and he's nothing more than a lonely old man."

"What do you think happened to him?" Ellery asks. "He lives in this big family home all by himself. There's a tragedy there. I'm convinced of it."

I clear my throat. "One mystery at a time, please."

"I have to agree with Ashlyn Dream on this. It's always better to focus your attention on one problem at a time before tackling the next problem."

"Why am I getting the middle name treatment?" I demand of Lilac.

She shrugs. "Why did I get it?"

I don't bother answering. It would be a waste of breath and time. And we've wasted enough time as it is. I check my watch. I don't have long before Rowan returns from the bakery. If I'm not back before him, he'll lose his dang mind. And while I love to drive the man crazy, I don't love when he denies me his pancakes for breakfast. I'm a sell-out for red velvet.

"Anyway," I holler and wait for everyone to quiet down before I continue, "As I was saying, I was reading Mercury's book about the history of Winter Falls, and I realized there's another building as old as the inn."

"By the way," Ellery interrupts to say, "I went through the rest of the boxes in the storage room after your search was called off."

Called off? Now, there's a unique way to say I was pulled away from the search by a grumpy bear before proceeding to trip over my own feet and break my ankle.

"Did you find anything?"

She shakes her head. "Sorry. Nothing. There weren't even any old newspaper clippings. Just boxes and boxes full of knick-knacks I now have to figure out a way to repurpose."

I shrug. "At least, we tried. Now, to the other building as old as the inn."

"I know you're referring to the building where the *Winter Falls Post* was located," Lilac says, "but the building is too young to help us in our search."

I cock an eyebrow. "It is?"

"Of course, it is. The *Winter Falls Post* was established in 1960 when the town of Winter Falls was founded. The Black Hat Bandit robbed the *Hastings National Bank* in February of 1955."

"And," Aspen adds, "his lover, Patricia, sent the letter about the hidden money in 1955, too."

I smirk. "Are all of you done proving you're wrong?"

Lilac purses her lips. "Wrong? I'm offended by your claim I'm wrong."

"It's not claiming when I can prove it," I sing.

She motions for me to go ahead.

I flourish Mercury's book about the history of the town and open it to the page I've marked. I set the book on the table and my sisters gather around me. I tap the picture of the former newspaper office, which now houses *Naked Falls Brewing*.

"Read the caption."

"The *Winter Falls Post* building was built in 1945 as the residence of Mr. and Mrs. Martin," Aspen reads out loud.

"Which means this building was around when Robert Adams, aka the Black Hat Bandit, was staying in Winter Creek."

"Winter Creek?" Juniper asks.

"It's what the settlement was named before the hippies arrived and renamed it Winter Falls."

Before Winter Falls became the first carbon neutral town in the world, it was a hippie commune. Mercury was one of the original settlers.

"What are you going to do with this information?" Ellery asks.

Aspen snorts. "We're going to the brewery to search for clues, of course."

I nod. "Exactly."

She wags at finger at me. "And you're not going without me."

I place a hand over my heart. "I wouldn't dare." Mostly because climbing ladders with a cast on is a bitch.

"Count me out," Ellery announces. "I haven't got time to be sifting through some other business's leftover crap."

Color me surprised. Not. If it weren't for me and the rest of my sisters, I doubt Ellery would ever leave the inn. I know it takes a lot to manage a successful business, but I have the feeling she's using work as a shield to hide. What is she hiding from, is the question.

"I haven't got time, either," Juniper adds.

Wow. Another big surprise. What is it with my sisters and their love of overworking?

"I have a deadline," Lilac says but doesn't explain more. She never does about her work. You'd think she was a nuclear engineer instead of an environmental engineer the way she keeps her work secret from everyone including her family.

Aspen throws her arm around my shoulders. "It's up to you and me, babycakes."

I glare at her. She knows I hate the nickname babycakes.

She winks. "This is going to be fun."

And a great excuse to escape the house and get away from the object of my every desire. Living with the sexy baker is driving me stark raving mad, especially since he's being nice to me after he discovered my secret business. Damn him. Can't he remain a grumpy jerk? It's easier to resist a jerk. Mostly.

Chapter 10

Sucker punch – to hit below the belt by revealing someone's secret to the whole dang town

ROWAN

I growl when Ashlyn jumps from the back of my golf cart. Damn stubborn woman won't let me help her at all. How am I supposed to ensure she doesn't get hurt on my watch again if she won't let me help her?

She hobbles toward the entrance of city hall on her crutches. When she reaches the stairs, I don't give her a chance to climb them. I pick her up and carry her into the building.

She slaps at my shoulders. "Let me down, Jeeves. I can handle things from here."

I snort in response. I know better than to engage in a discussion about her well-being with her. It leads down the path to jaw-clenching frustration. I've spent entirely too much time on that particular pathway lately.

Juniper waves from the front row where she's sitting with the rest of the West sisters. Before I can reach her, Petal stops me.

"Oh my." She fans her face. "Would you have a gander at this, girls?"

Suddenly, I'm surrounded by Feather, Sage, Cayenne, and Clove. None of them are a day under sixty and all of them have sex on the brain. I refer to them as the Gossip Gals. Not to their faces, of course. I'm not stupid.

"Ladies." I nod in their general direction.

"You can put me down now," Ashlyn grumbles.

"What's wrong, Ashlyn? You don't enjoy being carried around by the big, strapping football player?" Feather winks at me.

"I think the meeting is about to begin. We should probably find our seats," Ash suggests as she wiggles in my arms. I tighten my hold on her. If she thinks she can escape now that the gossip gals are in attendance, she's wrong.

"Please." Sage waves away her concern. "Forest wouldn't dare start a meeting without our go-ahead."

Forest is the current mayor. I wish I could say Sage is wrong, but these ladies are the unofficial royalty of Winter Falls, and Forest is merely the temporary mayor. He knows better than to upset them.

"Nonetheless, I want to make sure Ash is comfortable."

"I'd be more comfortable if you'd stop pretending to be some knight in shining armor and stop carting me around," Ash mutters under her breath.

"Ah." Clove places her hand over her heart. "He calls her Ash, and he wants her to be comfortable."

Shit. I stepped in it now, didn't I? The matchmakers will be placing their bets on when Ash and I will become a couple after this. I survey the room and notice almost everyone is studying our interaction. Double shit. The bets have already been placed.

I don't bother speaking again. There's no changing the minds of the residents of Winter Falls once the wagering has begun. I nod at the group of women before making my way to the front row.

Juniper slaps the empty seat on the end of the row. "Ashlyn can sit here."

I barely set her sister down before Juniper's shoving a bottle of beer in her hands. "Today's word is 'and'."

Ashlyn grins. "Awesome."

They clink bottles before taking their first sips. When Ash finishes drinking and licks her lips, I have to avert my gaze before the temptation to put my own lips on those lush ones of hers is too much.

Forest pounds the gavel at the front of the room. "Let's bring this monthly business meeting for the town of Winter Falls to order."

Mrs. West indicates the empty seat next to her in the row behind her daughters. "Sit with us, Rowan."

"Lookie, lookie, your paramour is sitting directly behind you, Ashlyn," Juniper teases.

Lilac twists in her seat to find who Juniper is referring to. When her eyes land on me, her nose scrunches. "I thought you said nothing happened between you two."

"Correct," Ash replies around a mouthful of popcorn.

Lilac sighs. "Juniper, your use of the word paramour is incorrect." Juniper sticks her tongue out at her.

Mrs. West leans close to whisper to me. "I don't know why you don't enjoy what Ashlyn is offering you," she says, and I nearly swallow my tongue. I may have grown up in Winter Falls and am used to all the open talk of sex, but I've never had a mom try to palm her daughter off on me before.

"Is it the age difference? Eight years won't matter much in the future. Besides, Ashlyn is a very mature twenty-three."

"I'm twenty-four now, Mom," Ash corrects her mom without turning around. "And I'd appreciate it if you didn't try to force men who don't even like me into dating me."

"You said the magic word. Drink!" Juniper nudges Ash's bottle of beer.

Bang! Bang! Bang!

"If we could have the attention of the West family now, so we can get this meeting started," Forest says from his position behind the table in front of the room.

"Go ahead." Mrs. West motions for him to begin.

"First order of business is the building next to *Naked Falls Brewing*. It's unsightly to have an empty storefront on Main Street. I'll now open the floor to suggestions for the space."

"You suck at picking the word of the day," Ashlyn grumbles to Juniper.

"There's no rule about not drinking unless someone says the word."

"Maybe not, but it's always fun to watch Uptight Number One and Uptight Number Two get tipsy."

"Drink!" Juniper cries and the row of sisters sip at their beers.

"Who's Uptight Number One and Uptight Number Two?" I ask.

Ash beams at me before yelling at her sisters to "Drink!"

Lilac sips from her beer and makes a face. "I thought we only had to drink when someone speaking on the floor said the word of the day."

Ash points to her. "Meet Uptight Number Two. Although she's more uptight than Uptight Number One." She gestures toward Aspen. "We've given big sis the number one spot since she's an old lady."

I frown. An old lady? Aspen is only two years older than me. Does Ash think I'm an old man? And why does the thought of her thinking I'm too old for her bother me? I'm not going to give into the temptation named Ash anyway.

"Sex shop!" Feather screams from somewhere behind me and reminds me now isn't the time to contemplate my non-relationship with Ash.

Forest sighs. "And who is going to manage this sex shop?"

The sisters in front of me drink in unison without any prompting. Ash holds up her empty bottle and Juniper hands her another one. I check the clock. We've barely been here fifteen minutes and she's finished her first beer already? She needs to slow down.

I lean forward to tell her to pump the breaks on her drinking, but Mrs. West grasps my arm and shakes her head at me. I sigh before slumping back in my seat.

Aspen stands. "What about a tourist shop for the town?"

Forest frowns. "Is the tourist shop in the bookstore not working out for you?"

When Aspen returned to Winter Falls, she had the idea of adding a tourist corner to her bookstore, *Fall Into A Good Book*. In addition to selling books about the area, she carries local products such as goat cheese from the local goat farm owned by her fiancé's brother and beer packages from the brewery. It's been a huge success as far I can tell.

Saffron, from whom Aspen bought the bookstore, stands. "And," she pauses to wait for the girls to drink, "it would be too much of a commitment for Aspen to manage both the bookstore and the tourist shop."

Aspen collapses back into her seat. "I didn't mean I'd manage it," she mumbles.

"Any other suggestions?" Forest asks.

Feather stands and he waves the gavel at her. "Other than a sex shop."

Feather is undeterred. "I don't know what's wrong with a sex shop. Soleil has gotten real good with knitting those vibrator covers she sells on Etsy."

"Knit vibrator covers?" Ellery glances over her shoulder to stare at Soleil. "Why don't I know about this?"

"Maybe because I already bought you one for Christmas," Aspen grumbles.

"Is it Christmas themed? Does it have mistletoe and Santa on it?"

I nearly choke on air. She wants a vibrator cover with Santa on it. What kind of weird obsession does she have with the jolly old man?

"Are you or Soleil prepared to operate the shop?" Forest asks.

"I already have a store," Feather pouts.

Soleil throws her hands in the air. "Don't look at me. My pottery classes are a hit with the tourists."

Suddenly, inspiration hits me, and I stand. "I have an idea."

Forest pounds his gavel again. "You have the floor, young man."

"What about a recording studio?" I ask and Ashlyn gasps.

"Recording studio? For rockstars? What kind of rockstars visit Winter Falls?"

"You'd be surprised," Juniper grumbles, and I nearly lose my train of thought. Are there seriously rockstars gallivanting around Winter Falls?

"No. Not for rockstars. I meant a recording studio for people to record other things. Maybe audiobooks."

"Audiobooks? Do you mean something similar to what Ashlyn narrates?" Sage asks, and Ashlyn springs to her feet.

She hops on her good foot, and I rush to hand her the crutches. Once she's stable, she addresses the crowd.

"Who else knows about my narrating?"

Every single person in the room raises their hand, including her parents and sisters.

"Why didn't anyone say anything?"

Mrs. West stands. "You seemed dead set on keeping it a secret. We figured there was a reason you wanted to keep the business private. I did try to guilt a confession out of you."

"You're not embarrassed about your work, are you?" Petal asks before Ash can respond to her mom. "Because it would be a shame if you stopped narrating." She fans her face. "Because you are good, girl. Real good."

"I second!" Sage raises her hand and soon every woman in the room has her hand raised.

"You've all listened to my audiobooks?" Ashlyn shrieks.

Forest bangs his gavel. "Let's bring this to a vote. Who's in favor of Ashlyn starting a recording studio?"

Hands shoot into the air.

"Wait!" Ash screams. "I never said I wanted to operate a recording business."

Forest ignores her. "The motion passes." *Bang!* "What's next on the agenda?"

"What's next on the agenda?" Ash mutters as she makes her way out of the room. "Why have an agenda when you're going to railroad people anyway?"

I hurry to catch up with her before she reaches the steps. I don't want her maneuvering on those steps when she's pissed. And she is beyond pissed. Lucky for me, she's mad at the whole town and not me for revealing her secret. Technically, I didn't reveal her secret. How was I to know everyone in town knew about her business?

Chapter 11

Rookie mistake – a mistake made by a woman who should know better

"Come on, Ash. You can't ignore me forever," Rowan yells through my bedroom door. Or, rather, *his* bedroom door since I'm stuck staying at his house despite my best efforts to escape.

My sisters – who normally can't reply to a chat message fast enough – suddenly have no time to answer me when I send them messages begging for help to move back home.

Aspen, I can understand. She thinks she's become some great matchmaker, now she's engaged. Juniper, I can also understand. She's got complete control of our apartment now. Well, she and her animals do. I didn't push Ellery too hard since she pushes herself hard enough already. But freaking 'has no emotions Lilac' could have helped me out at least. But no.

Which leaves me stuck in this beautiful home with an infuriating man who doesn't understand the word 'secret'.

"Watch me!" I yell back. Way to go, Ashlyn. Way to convince the man you're not some baby. "And my name's Ashlyn!" I insist instead of admitting how much I enjoy hearing Rowan call me by a name no one else uses.

I hear a thud and I imagine it's Rowan banging his forehead against the door in frustration. I'm intimately acquainted with the sound thanks to a dad who never 'got' me. I have to hand it to him. He did try. But he never understood why I wanted to grow up lightning fast and be my sisters' ages.

'Slow down,' he'd caution. 'You only get to be a kid once in your life.' Except when you're the baby of a family of five daughters. Then, apparently, you get to be 'babycakes' for-freaking-ever!

"You have to come out of there at some point!"

I do? I have everything I need in here. An unbelievable bathroom with a soaking tub, separate shower, dual sinks, and a toilet hidden behind a little door. Every surface is marble. It reminds me of a fancy hotel room. Or I assume it does. I've never stayed in a hotel room this fancy. Motels definitely don't have marble vanities.

In the bedroom itself is a California King sleigh bed. Of course, Mr. Former Pro Football Player has a California King for his entirely too huge and mouthwatering body. There's also a little sitting area near the bay window. The chairs are super comfy for reading. An activity I find myself doing on a regular basis since I now find myself with too much time on my hands.

And, finally, there's the walk-in closet. The closet is literally bigger than my bedroom in the apartment I share with Juniper. There's shelving on two sides with a comfy bench in the middle. There's even a little make-up area with a mirror, desk, and upholstered stool.

Best of all, the room is practically soundproof. I've been doing all of my recording in there. In fact, I'm way ahead on my narrating work. I need to find more work pronto. There's a limit to how many books a body can read. Unless such body is Aspen because she is a total book nerd.

"I made pancakes."

My ears perk up. "What kind of pancakes?"

"Is there any other kind than red velvet?"

There is, but no other pancakes are worth eating. Although, I bet Rowan could convince me otherwise. Damnit. No, he can't. Rowan is not to be trusted.

"Can I come in?"

Not even if you're carrying a breakfast tray with red velvet pancakes. Having Rowan in a room with a bed in it is in entirely too much temptation. It shouldn't matter. He treats me like I'm his little sister. But it does matter as I can't help imagining him sprawled out on the bed. Naked. Oh boy.

"No! I'll be out in a minute."

As soon as I cool off. Think unsexy thoughts, Ashlyn. A broken microphone. Bark Twain pooping all over the living room carpet and Meowise scampering through it and tramping feces all over the house. Cooling off is officially complete.

I grab a sweatshirt and throw it on over my pajamas. Fun fact. If you hardly go outside, there's no need to get dressed. Or wash your hair. I try smoothing down my hair. Amendment – you should totally wash your hair whether or not you go outside.

I hobble into the kitchen to find the table in the breakfast nook set. I nearly sigh at the sight. What I wouldn't give to have a set-up similar to this in my home. The kitchen is the wet dream of a chef, which makes sense since Rowan's a professional baker. And this little nook is set into a niche on the opposite side of the dining room. It's surrounded by windows with built-in bench seats.

It's the very definition of cozy. I can imagine myself sitting here drinking coffee with Rowan in the mornings. *No, Ashlyn. You can't. He thinks he's your big brother protector, remember?*

"What's this?" I ask when I notice a wooden box on the table.

Rowan flips it open. "Herbal teas. I didn't know which kind you wanted, so I got a whole variety."

"Did you buy every kind known to man?" I ask as I pick through the choices and decide on red bush tea.

"Does this mean you're speaking to me again?"

Oops. The vision of pancakes and tea made me temporarily forget my vow of silence. Not vow of silence as in I'm becoming a nun, but vow of silence as in I won't be speaking to Mr. Big Mouth Secret Teller anytime soon.

I grunt in response.

He sighs. "Fine. I'll speak. I'm sorry."

I raise an eyebrow. An apology needs to consist of more than the words 'I'm sorry'. There should be an explanation and groveling. Definitely groveling.

"I didn't think."

I snort. Tell me something I don't know.

"I mean. I guess I thought it would be a great business for you. A recording studio compliments your narration work perfectly."

Except I have no idea how to manage a recording studio *and* from the little – okay, fine, lot – of Googling I've done, it's way expensive to build a studio. To start with, there's soundproofing and all the digital equipment. On top of which, there's the building itself. The storefront next to the brewery has been vacant for a while. Who knows how the structure is holding up?

"And I don't want a sex shop across the street from my bakery."

"I don't know why not. Everyone knows sex gives you the munchies."

His eyes heat and I realize I not only opened my big, fat mouth, but I hit on him once again. But, wait a minute, why are his eyes heating? There goes my imagination running off again. Inventing responses I wish would happen when the truth is Rowan thinks of me as his little sister. Nothing more.

I return to my pancakes. Cream cheese frosting and chocolate have never let me down.

"Come on, Ash," he cajoles, and I grit my teeth before I end up forgiving him. I'm not ready to forgive him. Really, I'm not. "What's the big deal anyway? You said you aren't embarrassed by your work."

"And I'm not. There are other reasons for me to be mad about the situation besides being embarrassed."

He doesn't have the first clue, proving this man doesn't know me at all. I file the information away for times when I need to remind myself why Rowan and Ashlyn are not a good pair.

"I don't know what else the big deal could be."

"Maybe," I grit out, "the big deal is I wanted to choose the moment when I told the entire world about my business."

He shrugs and I see red. Seriously, a red haze covers my vision while my nostrils flare. I'm about to blow.

"The entire town of Winter Falls knew about your business already anyway."

"It doesn't mean I forgive you for spilling my secret."

"But is it really a secret if everyone already knew?" he asks, and my anger bursts out of me and I tell him things I never would if it weren't for the red haze thing.

"No one in this town takes me seriously. I'm always the little sister of the West girls. They call me babycakes and everyone laughs. And when they're not calling me baby, I'm 'the troublemaker sister'."

"I think you earned the designation."

I shove my palm into his face. "I'm talking now."

He motions for me to continue.

"For once, one freaking time, I wanted people in this town to sit up and pay attention to me. To take me seriously for a change. I wanted to present them with the finished feat of me, Ashlyn Dream West, as a successful business owner. But now, it's all ruined. All because of you," I snarl.

I run out of breath and wait for Rowan to respond with some placating words. After all, it's what happens every dang time I complain I'm not being taken seriously. But he doesn't react the way I think he will.

He palms my neck and uses his hold to draw me near before his mouth slams down on mine. I gasp in surprise, and he takes advantage of the opportunity to thrust his tongue into my mouth. He tastes of chocolate and coffee, and I want to drown in the flavor.

I clutch his t-shirt and drag him closer to me. The table stops our chests from being able to touch, but it doesn't prevent me from exploring his broad shoulders with my hands. The muscles I discover are hard and warm. Yum. I want to feel every hard inch of his naked skin.

Rowan rips his mouth away from mine with such intensity, I nearly tumble back into my chair. His hold on my neck is the only thing preventing me from melting to the floor in a big puddle of goo. He stares at me while he pants for breath for several moments before the intensity in his gaze shutters. Uh oh.

"This was a mistake."

"Didn't feel like a mistake to me."

He releases my neck and makes sure I'm steady in my seat before launching to his feet. "It was. We shouldn't... We can't... I can't ..." His hands dive into his hair, and he yanks on the strands.

"I don't know why not. I'm single. You're single. I'm an adult. You're an adult."

His hands drop. "No. We can't. I'm sorry."

He whirls around and sprints away, leaving me staring at his retreating form. Well, how's that for a shitty morning? I finally get my mouth on the object of my every desire, and he says it's a mistake. Well, fuck you very much, Rowan Aries Hansley.

Chapter 12

Full-court press – when everyone in your town decides to exert pressure on you to do as they wish; your wishes and desires be damned

ROWAN

I throw the dough onto the prep surface before pounding my fist into it. I'm such an idiot. I can't believe I gave into temptation and kissed Ashlyn, but when she talked about her goals for the future, I felt pride well up in me and I couldn't resist any longer.

Her lips were as soft as I'd imagined them, and her taste was even better than I imagined. She tastes of happiness, sunshine, and chocolate. An intoxicating flavor if ever there was one.

I pound the dough with my fist again. No! I need to stop these wayward thoughts of Ashlyn. I can never be with her. Replaying the kiss over and over in my mind is not going to change things.

"What did the dough ever do to you, amigo?"

I glance up at my assistant Bryan's question and scowl at him. He lifts his hands and backs away.

"Who pissed in your Cheerios?"

I snort. "I don't eat Cheerios."

He rolls his eyes before gasping and placing a hand on his chest. "Please tell me it finally happened."

I concentrate on kneading the dough. "What happened?"

"Don't insult me by pretending you don't know what I'm talking about."

I shrug and keep my eyes on my dough. Hopefully, he'll drop the subject and move on. He hops onto the prep table. I guess not. I shove him off. He squeals as he pretends to fall off. Such a drama queen.

"This is beyond exciting. Who do I tell first?" He claps and dances around the room.

I slam my palms down on the table. "No one. You tell no one."

"Oh. You're having an illicit affair. Don't worry. I can keep a secret."

I know he can. After all, he's kept the secret of what happened with my ex-wife from the town. And, in this town, keeping a secret is akin to a miracle.

"Nothing happened."

"Grumpy face doesn't say nothing happened."

"I need to finish baking the bread for the morning rush."

He crosses his arms over his chest and leans against the wall. "You should probably get to telling me what happened pronto then, shouldn't you?"

I debate throwing his ass out into the alley behind the bakery. I can do it. Bryan is at least half a foot shorter than me and a good fifty pounds lighter.

He wags his finger at me. "Don't you dare try it, me amigo. I'm liable to cry in pain when you throw me, and the police station is next door."

I grunt. I hate when he's right.

He frowns. "Was it not good? Was it not everything you imagined?"

Damnit. I hate how he knows about the feelings I've been harboring for Ashlyn for the past year since she returned home from college. I should know better than to open the good whiskey when he's around. For reasons I've yet to understand, he can get me to confess my deepest, darkest secrets.

It made him a great personal assistant when I was playing football. I thought when I returned to Winter Falls, he'd find another football player to assist. Wrong. The guy heard about my plans to open a bakery and nearly wet his pants in excitement. He couldn't follow me back to Winter Falls quick enough.

I need to get confession time over with or I really will be late with this morning's bread.

"We kissed," I grit out.

"Was it not good?" He squints his eyes as he studies me. I count to five. One. Two. Three. Four. Five. His eyes light up and he bounces on his toes. "It was better than you imagined."

I grunt.

"I take your grunt as a yes. What's the problem?"

I glare at him. "You know what the problem is."

Actually, he doesn't. He thinks he knows all about what happened between my ex-wife and me, but there's one little tidbit of information I kept to myself. No one needs to know about my secret shame.

He rolls his eyes. "You need to get over yourself. Being unable to keep Mrs. Gold Digger happy, doesn't mean you can't make another woman happy."

If I couldn't keep Sandra happy with all my millions while I was a pro-football player, how can I possibly make Ash happy while I'm a simple hometown baker?

Bryan sighs. "I think I need to revise my bet. You're more stubborn than I initially calculated."

"You're betting on my relationship with Ash?"

"Of course, I am. There aren't any inside information laws in Winter Falls."

The bell over the door of the bakery rings and Bryan snaps to. "Get your bread done. The morning rush is about to begin."

He sashays out of the kitchen into the café, and I return to my bread. Hopefully, the interrogation is now over.

I finish the bread and put the mini loaves onto a tray. When I step into the front, it's organized chaos. Every table is full, and the line stretches out the door. Saturday mornings are usually busy, but this is ridiculous. I place the tray in the display before joining Bryan to help the customers.

"Finally!"

I glance over my shoulder to find out who yelled and nearly groan when I realize it's Sage. She's the police dispatcher and prides herself on knowing all of the gossip in town before anyone else.

I force a smile on my face. "Hi, Sage. Did you need me?"

Her constant companion, Feather, gives me the once-over before licking her lips. "If she doesn't need you, I certainly do."

She's joking. I hope. Feather's nearly old enough to be my grandmother.

"And to think, I changed the diaper on this strapping young man." Sage sighs.

I feel my cheeks warm. It's always a little awkward when someone who babysat you leers at you.

"Ladies, ladies." Bryan throws his arm around me. "The big, burly footballer is all mine for the next," he checks the clock, "seven hours."

"Where do I sign up for the following seven hours?" Cayenne asks.

"Don't you have a yoga class to teach?" Is it too much to ask for the female business owners of this town to actually work at their businesses instead of gossiping at my bakery?

"Yoga class is finished," Aspen announces from behind me.

I study her disheveled appearance. "Hot yoga?"

"I wish," she grumbles. "Apparently, hot yoga is limited to the summer months and not the fall months when I wouldn't mind a hot room as much."

I waggle my eyebrows at her. "Chief Alston not keeping you warm enough at night?"

Next to her, Ellery groans. "No. Just no. I don't need anymore play by plays of their sexy times." She does appear a bit green about the gills at the idea.

"I don't know why not." Lilac appears confused. It's her standard face whenever human interaction is involved. "I thought you were happy Aspen and Lyric are back together and engaged."

The whole town is happy Aspen and Lyric are back together. The two have only had eyes for each other since high school. Their break-up after college rocked the core of this town. I'm glad they found their way back to each other. They deserve their happiness.

Despite my being two years younger than them, we've been friends for years. Lyric and I played football together back in the day. I thought he'd lose it when I joined the team my freshman year and won the varsity quarterback position he'd had for the two previous years. The guy was nearly as good a quarterback as I was. He could have gone pro if he wanted, but all he wanted was to become a cop in our hometown, and it almost cost him the love of his life.

"Whatever," Ellery grumbles. "I want your sweetest most decadent cupcake."

"How's Ashlyn doing?" Juniper asks.

I narrow my eyes at her. She had to mention Ashlyn in front of the town's Gossip Gals aka Feather, Sage, and Cayenne. At least Petal and Clove aren't around

My glare has no effect on Juniper. She smirks up at me. "Do you have any of those red velvet pancakes? I hear they're divine."

The little shit. She knows I don't serve the pancakes at the bakery, but I've made them for her sister.

"I need to get back to the ovens."

Bryan bars my entrance to the kitchen. "I've got it." He winks before twirling around.

I'm regretting hiring him to assist me in the bakery right now. But I have options. He's not from around here. No one will miss him if he disappears. The hills around the town are empty. No one would find his body.

"Don't think I don't know you're picking out a shovel to bury me with," he sings from inside the kitchen loud enough for the entire bakery to hear him.

"Poor Bryan. He works his little behind off here and what does he get? Rowan being mean to him." Feather tuts at me to show her disappointment in me.

"I'm not mean to him." At least, not when anyone's around.

Sage elbows her way to the front of the line. "What's this about red velvet pancakes?"

Juniper has no trouble telling her everything. "Apparently, he bakes Ashlyn red velvet pancakes every morning."

"Not every morning."

She smirks. "Ah, so you admit to making breakfast for my little sister."

I frown. "Don't call Ashlyn your little sister."

Ashlyn hates to be reminded of how she's younger than all of her sisters. It's more than being uncomfortable with their teasing. She actually believes no one takes her seriously. I'll take her seriously.

"He's sticking up for her and his heart rate is elevated," Lilac points out.

I cross my arms over my chest and glare down at her.

"What? I'm merely pointing out the obvious."

Aspen sighs. "We've had this conversation, Lilac. You're not allowed to point out when it's evident someone is physically aroused."

Lilac frowns. "I didn't say he was physically aroused. Men usually have an erection if they're aroused." She leans over the counter as if she's going to check if I have a hard-on.

I don't, although the thought of Ashlyn makes my blood pump quicker through my body. Especially now since I know how she tastes.

Aspen claps. "This is too much fun."

I hear the sound of something falling in the kitchen. Thank god. "Sorry ladies. I need to check on Bryan," I say and rush out of there like my pants are on fire.

Chapter 13

Take it on the chin – to suffer all the blows thrown at you because you're a complete idiot

"Where are we going?" I ask Rowan as we travel in his golf cart toward Main Street.

This morning, I woke to a tray of red velvet pancakes sitting outside my bedroom door. I may be mad – no, furious – at the man, but I'm not an idiot. Besides, we don't waste food in Winter Falls. I gobbled down those pancakes before showering and taming my hair.

An hour into recording, I realized I needed some herbal tea to soothe my throat if I was going to be able to narrate without resembling a croaking toad. Let me tell you, croaking toads are not sexy. The minute I entered the kitchen, Rowan herded me outside toward his golf car.

He grunts instead of answering my question, but I'm getting to the point where I can interpret his grunts. This one means *I'm not telling you.* Figures.

The golf cart slows before coming to a stop in front of the brewery. "Oh, hell no," I announce before jumping from the cart and crutching my way toward the brewery, which I'm positively certain is not our end destination.

Rowan steps onto the sidewalk in front of me and bars my movement. "Wrong way."

I feign surprise. "What? You're not treating me to lunch at the brewery?" I curl my bottom lip in a pout. "But I'm hungry."

"You can't possibly be hungry. You literally ate six pancakes less than an hour ago."

I know. My stomach is bloated, and the idea of food makes me want to barf, but the idea of discussing building a recording studio business with anyone – let alone Mr. You're a Mistake Hansley – makes me want to projectile vomit. I'm choosing the lesser of two evils here.

"Come on. It won't hurt to survey the building."

Wrong. It will hurt worse than breaking my ankle to discuss working on a business with the man who thinks I'm a mistake. Grrr... How can something, which felt like heaven be a mistake? Unless it didn't feel like heaven to him. I'd rather take a dagger to the heart than hear him air those thoughts.

"I don't know why you're involved with this," I scream at him.

"Good question," Eden says.

I survey the area to discover the entire town watching us. Great. Every single resident of Winter Falls is here to enjoy my confrontation with Rowan. At least, there aren't any tourists around. Tourist season is mostly over, although Winter Falls continues to get a fair amount of tourists during the mild weather weekends.

Rowan raises an eyebrow and nods toward the empty storefront. I glare at him even as I begin moving in that direction. Jerk. He knows I don't want everyone knowing about my business. As in my money-making business, not my personal business. I know better than to expect the people of Winter Falls to keep their noses out of my personal business.

Rowan fishes a key out of his pocket and unlocks the door with it. I enter the store and study the interior. The swap shop used to be located here, but it shut down because it didn't make enough money to pay the lease. Big surprise. Not charging any money for people to swap clothes doesn't exactly earn any cold, hard cash.

Winter Falls may have commenced life as a hippie commune, but the chamber of commerce won't let someone occupy a storefront on Main Street without paying the monthly rent. They're not ruthless about it. They'll barter and let people fall a few months behind on their payments, but even hippies have a limit to their patience.

"The clothing racks are easy to deal with."

"They are? You know you can't throw them away."

"Yes, Ash, I'm aware. I grew up in Winter Falls, too, you know. I found an online website for store supplies. We can sell the clothing racks and all the rest of it there." He motions to the dressing rooms and check-out counter.

He slaps a hand against the outside wall. "The structure is sound. You don't need to worry about the bones of the building."

I snort. "Just soundproof the entire thing and build recording booths."

"I already talked to Orion. He said soundproofing doesn't have to be expensive."

I glare at him. "You talked to Petal's husband without consulting me?"

"Who else was I going to talk to? Orion is the only handyman in town. I can help since I did a lot of the reconstruction in my house myself. And I know Lyric is pretty handy, too."

"Don't ask my dad to help out. I still trip on the kitchen floor every time I'm in there."

He nods and rubs his hands together. "Great. The plan is set. We'll start with sound—"

I throw up a hand to stop him. "No, you big oaf. We do not have a plan."

"We can build the booths first if you prefer. In fact, it might be a good idea. Okay. New plan. We'll build the booths and soundproof them."

Is he deliberately being obtuse?

"Stop!" I screech. "Stop with all your plans and scheming. I never agreed to this whole recording studio thing. I'm perfectly happy narrating my audiobooks in your walk-in closet."

"But what about when your ankle is healed, and you move back home?"

Ouch! He had to remind me of my temporary place in his life, didn't he? As if I don't remember him saying kissing me was a mistake and walking away.

Whereas he seems to have forgotten the encounter, I can't stop thinking about our kiss. The memory occupies every waking moment. And, when I'm not awake, I dream of his lips on mine. And the dream doesn't stop with a simple kiss, no matter how hot the actual kiss was. No, in my dreams, Rowan's lips explore my entire body. I nearly shiver at the idea of being naked and laid out for him.

It will never happen, though. Rowan made his intentions or lack thereof perfectly clear. My dreams of a happily ever after with him are just that – dreams. Little girl fantasies. And I'm sick and tired of being the little girl.

"When I move back home," I tell him, "I will use the closet in my apartment the way I've been doing since I returned to Winter Falls last year."

"I thought you said my walk-in closet is bigger than your entire bedroom."

Rub it in, Mr. Money Banks, why don't you?

"Not all of us have millions from our years of playing professional football," I snarl. "And yet we manage to have fun and fulfilling lives."

He rubs the back of his neck. "I didn't mean to sound like a rich asshole."

"Well, congratulations, you did."

He grunts. This one means *let me talk, woman.*

I roll my eyes and motion for him to speak.

"This recording studio could be a good business for you. An additional income on top of what you're earning from your narration work."

"You don't get it, do you?"

"Explain it to me."

"I'll do you one better. I'll mansplain it."

To his credit, he doesn't growl at me for talking down to him.

"Go ahead."

"I. Do. Not. Want. A. Recording. Studio."

"Why the hell not?" He explodes.

Because I don't want the entire town to witness my failure, I think but don't say. This man has already heard enough about my self-doubt, I'm not giving him another piece more of me. Mistake, I remind myself. He thinks I'm a mistake.

"Could I record my audiobooks at the studio? Yes, yes, I could. But I'd also have to do a whole lot more. I'd need to attract customers. From where? No freaking clue. I'd have to be on-site to grant these non-existent customers access to the location. On top of everything, there's all the other shit involved in having a business. Spreadsheets and P&L statements. The list goes on and on."

"Can I speak now?"

"If you must."

His lips tip up in an almost smile before he clears his throat and tackles my problems one by one.

"First, the easy stuff. The so-called business 'shit'. It's all stuff you do now anyway."

"Yeah, but—"

He holds up his hand. "No. It's my turn to speak now."

"Whatever."

"Access to the location is a no-brainer. You can put a lock with a code system on the door. Each customer gets their own code."

Damn. I hadn't thought of that.

"As far as attracting customers, I'll help."

I narrow my eyes at him. "Help how?"

He shrugs. "I have a lot of contacts."

And there he goes shoving his fame in my face again. Reminding me how I will never be good enough for him.

"I don't want your contacts."

"Too bad. I'm going to help you whether you want me to or not."

I cock an eyebrow at him. "Oh yeah?"

He fists his hands on his hips. "Oh yeah."

"Have fun. Because I'm not getting involved," I declare before hippity hopping my way out of the building.

I'm fuming the entire time I make my way across and down the street to *The Inn on Main* where I know Ellery keeps chocolate chip cookies stashed for emergencies. How dare he think he can railroad me into establishing a business I don't want? Why the hell would I want to work on a project with him? I'm just a mistake after all.

A freaking mistake. Kissing Rowan was the single best moment I've ever had with a man in my entire life, and he considers it a mistake. I'll show him a mistake.

Chapter 14

Keep the ball rolling – go in search of the next clue in a mystery

"Hey, Ashlyn Bashlyn," Moon greets as I enter *Naked Falls Brewing* with Aspen.

After we hug, I introduce Aspen. "You remember my sister, Aspen."

Her cheeks darken. "You bet I do. It's hard to forget the first time you observe people who aren't your parents or on the movie screen having a romantic encounter."

Aspen groans next to me. "Could you try to forget?"

Moon giggles. "Are you kidding? I need some images for my lady spank bank." She sighs. "Although, since you and Lyric are back together, I'm certain I'll have some new material soon." She winks.

"But now we're adults and have a house with a bed and don't need to sneak around at the river," Aspen tells her.

Moon barks out a laugh. "Please. I know you went skinny dipping with Lyric this past weekend."

"Why did I want to come back to this town again?" Aspen mutters.

"Because it's awesome," I remind her.

"Do you two want a table for lunch?" Moon cranes her neck to peer behind us. "And where are the rest of the West sisters? Do I need to prepare the fire extinguisher?"

"Maybe if Rowan shows up. When he's in the same room as Ashlyn, sparks fly. Whoosh!"

I glare at her. "Sparks do not fly."

She laughs and gestures toward my face. "Wrong. They're flying out of your eyes right now."

I ignore her to reply to Moon. "We don't need a table. We need a favor."

Moon motions us to the little alcove near the hostess station. "Tell me more. What kind of favor? Are we playing a prank on someone? I still have some ipecac syrup from the time when—"

I slap a hand over her mouth before she can give away all my secrets. The act causes me to lose my balance and I tilt forward on my way to falling flat on my face.

Aspen steadies me. "Actually, we're here about something else."

Moon cocks her eyebrow.

"We need to find out if there are any old boxes from before the building was a brewery," I explain.

"You mean from when the *Winter Falls Post* was in circulation?"

"Yes," I agree, although we're searching for something older. I don't fill her in on the mystery, though. I trust Moon with my life, but she does have a tendency to blurt things out. She nearly told Aspen about the whole ipecac incident less than two minutes ago after all.

Moon wiggles her nose as she thinks about it. "I don't know about any boxes, but there is an old safe."

"An old safe?"

"Yeah. You know one of those old-fashioned safes people used to have embedded in the walls of their houses."

I don't know anything about old-fashioned safes people used to have in their houses. What I do know is we're searching for a clue from before this building was a newspaper. Could this safe contain the answer to our questions? If I could bounce on my toes, I would.

"Have you cracked the safe?" Aspen asks.

"Me?" Moon snorts. "Not hardly."

Next to me, I hear Aspen grind her teeth. "Let me rephrase. Has the safe been opened?"

"Yeah, Miller and Elder hired some guy off the internet to open it up. They thought they'd find some loot, or I don't know what in there."

Loot? Do Miller and Elder, the out-of-town owners of the brewery, know about The Mystery of the Black Hat Bandit's Missing Loot? Is the mystery why they decided to locate their business here? Why they pushed and pushed to establish a business in a town where out-of-towners need permission from the chamber of commerce to establish a business?

"And?" Aspen leans forward. "Did they find anything?"

"Not really." Moon shakes her head. "Just a bunch of old papers. Deed for the house and other boring stuff."

"Deed for the house?" Aspen's eyes sparkle and I know she's got a plan. Great. My plan was basically to stroll in here and ask around. I'll admit it wasn't my most brilliant plan.

She clears her throat. "Actually, as the person who's in charge of the town's tourist center, boring old papers is why we're here. We're hoping to get more information about the history of the town."

"Yeah," I agree, warming up to her idea. "Mercury's book about the history of the town centers on his own experiences. We need a less biased picture."

Listen to me. I sound like I know what I'm doing.

"I doubt the guys will mind if you have a peek at the documents. Come on." Moon motions us toward the door marked 'employees only'.

We follow her as we pass the kitchen, the breakroom, and a storage room until we enter a second storage room. She leads us to the back of the room where there's a safe built into the wall. She pulls the door open to reveal a stack of papers.

"Why don't Miller and Elder use the safe? They can't remove it from the wall without damaging the structure of the building anyway."

There's a slight possibility someone may have been doing a bit of research on renovating houses as of late. I'm not going to agree to renovate the storefront next door to make a recording studio. I'm not. I'm merely obsessed with home renovation shows is all.

"What would they need a safe for? There's hardly any cash at the end of the night as most people pay with their bank cards anyway."

Oh, right. I should have realized.

Moon checks the time on her phone. "Shoot. I need to get back. My tips live or die by the swiftness of my service." She dashes out without a backwards glance.

As soon as she's gone, I hiss at Aspen. "Do you think Miller and Elder know about the missing loot from the bank robbery?"

She wrinkles her nose at me. "What makes you ask?"

"Moon said they were searching for loot."

"Moon also has an overactive imagination."

I can't deny it. She's my best friend, but she does tend to exaggerate a lot. Take the time we stalked … er… ran into Aspen and Lyric at the river. They were just kissing, but Moon talks as if they were having full on sex. Ew. I don't want to watch my sister having sex.

"Take a load off." Aspen motions to a box and I sit down. She grabs half of the papers from the safe and dumps them in my lap. When I don't immediately dive into reviewing them, she taps the top sheet. "What are you waiting for? Get to reading."

"Yes, ma'am. Whatever you say, ma'am."

She ignores my sarcasm. Truth be told, she has a whole lot of experience since – according to our mother – I came out of the womb being sarcastic. I don't know how a baby can be sarcastic, but I've learned to let my mom's words glide off of my back.

Aspen takes a spot on the floor next to the safe and begins sorting through her pile. I scan the top document. An old copy of a receipt for services rendered. Boring. The next document isn't much more interesting. *Buy eggs.* I throw the paper on the ground next to the first one.

"Oh my god!" Aspen squeals.

I freeze as I wait for someone to rush into the room at her shout. When no one comes crashing through the door I hiss at her, "Shush. Do you want everyone to know about the mystery?"

"Sorry, but you have to see this." She waves an envelope at me.

"It's sealed. What are you excited about?"

"Read to whom it's addressed."

"To Patricia," I read aloud. "Patricia? As in Patricia Hall? As in the black hat bandit's lover?"

"There's one surefire way to find out," Aspen says as she slips her finger beneath the flap of the envelope. She stops with her finger poised there.

"What are you waiting for? Do it already?"

"You're too much fun to tease," she says but she does finally open the envelope. "It's a letter."

I grab the letter from her and begin reading out loud. "To my love Patricia. If you are reading this letter, then I am either no longer on this earth or I am indisposed." I stop to snort. "Indisposed? I think he means prison."

"Or he's on the lam," Aspen remarks.

"Did they use the term 'on the lam' in the 1950s?"

"Who cares?" She taps the letter. "Continue reading."

"In any event, I've done as you asked." I pause again. "Done as she asked? What does he mean?"

"Let me think." Aspen taps her chin. "Hold on. I took a picture of Patricia's letter to Robert with my phone." She fishes her phone out of her pocket and scans the letter. "Here it is. I think he means the postscript. It says I hope you hid the money well."

My eyes widen. "Son of a gun! He's telling her he hid the money."

"But where?" Aspen asks.

"You'll find the item referred to in the temporary tablecloth." I pause reading again. "Obviously, the item is the money. But what does he mean with temporary tablecloth?"

"No idea. What else does it say?"

"I long to hold you in my arms again. Yada yada yada. I love you. Blah blah blah. Nothing else about the loot."

"Let me see." Aspen snatches the letter from me to read it for herself. She scans it and frowns. "You're right. There's nothing else here."

"I told you so."

The door bangs open, and I nearly fall off my box in surprise.

"Sorry, Ashlyn. The bosses are kind of mad I let you back in here without supervision." Moon shrugs.

"It's fine," I say and stand. "We're done anyway."

"Did you find anything interesting?"

I stand in front of Aspen as she shoves the letter down her pants. "Nope," I deny. "You were right. Boring stuff."

She motions to the door. "Bummer. Are you off to home now?"

"I think you mean Rowan's house," Aspen says, and I reach back to pinch her. And people say I'm the troublemaker in the family.

Moon, bless her heart, ignores Aspen. "Or do you have time for a beer? I have a break coming up."

"I have time for a beer." No one's waiting on me to come home anyway.

It sounds lovely – a man waiting for me at home. It would be even more lovely if the man were Rowan. But after he said our kiss was a mistake, I know it will never happen. Damnit, Ashlyn. You need to get over him and move on. Easier said than done.

Chapter 15

Fair Play – to respect the rules as long as you're the one making up the rules

ROWAN

"Where are we going?" Ash asks from the rear of my golf cart.

"I told you. To get a bite to eat. I don't feel like cooking."

"I can cook. Or we can order in."

And let her go hide in her bedroom to eat again? No way. I'm done with her avoiding me. We need to clear the air because I'm not living with the woman who drives me absolutely crazy scurrying out of every room I walk into.

I realize I'm being a hypocrite. It would be easier all around if I let Ash ignore me. We can never be anything other than friends. But I can't do it. I know she's hurting and it's my fault. I should have never kissed her. Except our kiss was the best kiss of my life.

When I park the golf cart in front of the brewery, Ash rears back.

"Nope. Not happening. I am not discussing the recording studio with you. Take me away, Jeeves!"

I wave toward the recording studio where the windows are now covered with newspaper so no one can peer inside. "You don't need to worry. Someone else is busy with the store now."

She glares at the building for a long moment before nodding. Hurdle one has been crossed and no one was injured. Onto the next hurdle.

I go to help her out of the golf cart, but she brandishes one of her crutches like it's a sword.

"No. I got this."

I fist my hands as she jumps off of the cart. She wobbles as she lands and I step closer, but she growls at me. I hold up my hands.

"Let's get this over with," she mutters as we make our way to the entrance of the brewery restaurant.

When I open the door, the noise hits me. "I didn't think it'd be this crowded."

Ash snorts. "What did you expect? There are exactly two restaurants in Winter Falls. They're always crowded."

I waggle my eyebrows. "Rumor has it there's an excellent bakery in town, too."

She rolls her eyes.

The waitress rushes up to us. "Ashlyn Bashlyn! Twice in one week. I guess you haven't forgotten your bestie now you're a famous narrator after all."

Ashlyn groans. "Shut it, Moon."

Moon sticks out her hand. "You must be Rowan. I'm Moon. Ashlyn's BFF."

BFF? Do people still use that term? And why is she introducing herself? I know Moon. She was practically surgically attached to Ashlyn when they were teenagers.

She wiggles the hand she's still sticking out, and I grasp it. She uses my hand to drag me forward.

"I have a table all ready for you," she whispers and winks.

She drops my hand and whirls around. "Follow me."

I place a hand on Ashlyn's lower back as I follow her to our table. She shivers at my touch and it's official. I'm a complete asshole. I know I can't have her, but I can't help myself from touching her every chance I get anyway. It's not fair to her, and I need to stop.

"Here we are!" Moon announces when we reach a table in the corner. A private table where the eyes of most of Winter Falls can't watch us. Great. Moon thinks we're here for a romantic meal.

Ashlyn takes a seat, but I stand there trying to think of an excuse to switch to a less private table. Moon isn't having it. She pushes me and I stumble into a chair.

"I'll be back for your order soon," she announces before skipping away.

"You have interesting friends," I tell Ash as I watch Moon leave.

"She's a bit abrasive at first, but she's got a heart of gold," she says before picking up her menu and using it to cover her face.

She's hiding again and I don't like it one bit. I reach over and pull the menu down. I grunt at her and she rolls her eyes.

"I'm not hiding."

She's lying, but I let it go. Time to get to the tough stuff. I clear my throat.

"We need to talk."

She slams her menu down on the table. "I cannot believe you, Rowan Aries Hansley. You did not bring me here to have 'the talk'. How cliché can you get?"

There goes any hope of having a calm discussion. Ashlyn Dream West doesn't do calm, but I thought being in a public place would discourage her from yelling at me. I'm an idiot. Nothing discourages my girl from telling you what's on her mind.

Before I can open my mouth and try again, Sage waltzes by our table. She's breathing hard and her face is red as if she's been running. She probably has been. My bet is she heard Ash and I were having dinner here and she ran over here from the police station as fast as she could.

"Ashlyn West! It's good to see you out. How are you doing?"

"What do you want?" Ash asks instead of engaging in small talk with her.

Sage's lips purse. "Someone's awful grumpy." She turns to me. "Are you not taking good care of our girl?"

I can take more than good care of Ash. Our kiss was merely the tip of the iceberg. I want to lay her out and feast from her like she's a meal made especially for me. My pants tighten at the thought. I shake my head. Shit. No. Ash isn't meant for me.

"Ash can fend for herself."

Sage leans close, but Moon yells her name before she can speak again. "I heard Chief Alston is wondering where you are."

Sage throws her hands in the air. "He probably can't find the filters for the coffee machine." She sighs. "Duty calls."

After she wanders off, Moon winks at us. "You're welcome."

"I wonder what gossip Sage will invent about us." Ash taps her chin. "Of course, the whole town now knows we're here, so she doesn't need to invent anything."

I scan the room and notice how everyone in the place is focused on us. I glare at them, and they drop their gazes. Maybe bringing Ash to a public location to have our talk wasn't the best idea I've ever had.

"I wonder what the current bet is at. I should get in on it," Ash ponders.

"You can't bet about yourself. It's unfair."

She waves away my concern. "As if 'fair' is ever an issue in this town. The bet could be my revenge for them railroading me about the recording studio."

"But you aren't interested in launching a recording studio business," I remind her.

Her brow wrinkles and her nose scrunches. "True. Is it truly railroading if they failed in their endeavors?"

Moon plops two beers down on our table. "This is the Autumn Equinox IPA. You'll love it. Have you decided what you want to eat?"

I haven't even picked up my menu yet. "What do you recommend?"

She taps her chin as she studies me. "You're a big guy. For you, I'd recommend the half-pounder burger. The caramelized onion marmalade is made with the *Naked Falls Brewing* blonde beer, and it's served with Belgian fries."

"Sounds good," I say and hand her my menu.

"I'll have one, too," Ash says, and I cock my eyebrow at her. "Shut it, you. I know my ass is too big, but I'm not going to starve myself."

I frown. I don't want her to starve herself. I have first-hand knowledge of how it is to live with a woman who starves herself. It's the furthest thing from pleasant. Every meal becomes a discussion. And, if you dare to say anything about her eating habits, an argument is certain to follow.

"Your ass is fine."

She frowns. She thinks I'm placating her, but I can't tell her what I actually think of her ass. How it's the perfect size for my hands while I pound into her from behind. Damnit. I need to stop imagining this woman I can never have naked. I'm trying to protect both of us.

"As I was saying, we need to talk."

"If you give me the 'it's not you, it's me speech', I will stab you in your eye with this fork and I won't regret it one bit." She lifts up her fork and makes little stabbing motions to demonstrate.

I play along and cover my eyes. It's a good excuse to buy myself some time to readjust what I'm going to say because I was going to give her the 'it's me, not you' speech. But I know better now. Duly noted.

"I need to apologize."

Her eyes widen to the size of saucers. "Apologize? You're going to apologize for sticking your tongue down my throat?"

"I don't want you to feel uncomfortable in my home or think your stay there is contingent on us having some type of fling."

Her eyes flare for a second, but she blinks and douses the fire. "Rowan, let me say this in as simple words as I possibly can, what are you thinking?"

I open my mouth to answer, but she's not done talking.

"I am more than aware of how my staying with you is not contingent on anything. If my stay were contingent on us having a fling, you wouldn't have kissed me before saying the kiss was a mistake."

Damn. She thinks I didn't enjoy the kiss. Truth is. It was the best kiss of my life. I can't tell her what I think, though. I won't lead her on when there can be nothing between us.

"I—"

Ash interrupts again and I'm glad since I have no idea what I was going to say.

"It's okay. We can forget about the kiss. We'll pretend it never happened."

As if I could ever forget how her lips felt on mine. But I smile and nod as if the idea of pretending the kiss never happened doesn't cause me to want to drag her into my arms and give her a kiss she will never be able to forget.

Our stare-down is interrupted by Moon arriving at our table. She leans close to whisper, "Are you guys done with 'the talk' now? I didn't want to ruin your meal."

"We're done," Ash says, and I fear she means with more than our discussion.

Shit. I made things worse, didn't I? This is why I can't have a woman. I can't make her happy.

Chapter 16

Square off – to assume the position of someone about to fight off a whole bunch of gossiping ladies

"Yeah! She's here," Petal screams when I enter *Fall Into A Good Book* for the monthly book club.

Nope. I can't do this. I whirl around, intent on making a quick exit, but Moon shoves me into the bookstore. She follows me in and closes the door behind us.

"What are you doing?" I hiss. "You don't read."

"I read."

I raise an eyebrow. "Anything other than the back of a cereal box?"

She gasps and places a hand over her heart. "As if I'd ever buy cereal in a box!"

Aspen arrives and drags me away. "Stop gabbing and get your butt over here."

She helps me to a solitary seat facing the rest of the group of chairs. "What's going on? Why am I being seated in front like I'm about to give a lecture?"

"You seriously didn't think you could come out of the closet about your audiobook narrating and we wouldn't want to hear all about it."

"I think you're confused about what coming out of the closet means," I grumble to her.

"Yeah, Ashlyn. We want to hear all about how you get in the mood to narrate porn," Feather says.

"Do you use anyone for inspiration?" Petal waggles her eyebrows.

Moon's hand shoots into the air. "I know who she uses for inspiration." I glare at my former best friend. She snickers. "Please, I'm not revealing secrets when the whole world knows about your crush on Rowan."

"I want to hear why Ashlyn tried to keep this a secret from her family," Mom asks.

Crap. Mom's here. And we're going to talk about me narrating erotic romances. This won't be embarrassing. Not at all.

Sage rolls her eyes. "As if you can keep a secret in this town. She should have known better."

I cross my arms over my chest. "How did everyone find out anyway?" I glare at Juniper.

She lifts her palms up. "I swear I didn't tell anyone."

"How did everyone find out?"

"It wasn't hard," Sage claims.

I'm beginning to wonder why Lyric employs her as the police dispatcher. Aren't police supposed to use discretion? And not tell everyone in town who's getting in trouble? Can I lodge some type of complaint?

"You probably shouldn't have used the name of your first cat for the first name of your stage name," Cayenne says.

Traitor. It'll be a cold day in hell before I attend one of her yoga classes again.

"What were you doing? Going through all the names of audiobook narrators? You have too much time on your hands."

"Are we going to continue this charade or tell her how we figured it out?" Lilac asks. Ellery slaps her arm. "What? No one warned me there would be lying this evening."

"It's not lying," Ellery hisses. "We're teasing her is all."

Lilac's brow wrinkles. "I don't understand. Is this similar to sarcasm?"

Having an older sister who doesn't understand basic human emotions can be annoying sometimes but not now.

"Lilac!" I call to gain her attention. When her gaze lands on me, I ask, "How did everyone find out?"

"When you weren't home to receive a package, your neighbor, Soleil, took it for you." I find Soleil in the crowd. She blushes and avoids my gaze. I think I'm beginning to understand what happened.

"She noticed the package was a microphone and a pop filter. She asked Sage what you use a pop filter for and—"

I raise my hand to stop her. "I get it."

"There's more to the story," Lilac insists because she believes you should have every single detail of a story before you can make a factual assessment. I don't need to assess the story. I know what happened. The people of Winter Falls snooped until they figured out my secret. Typical really.

Aspen shoves a glass of wine in my hand. "You're going to need this."

I'm afraid to ask why. Instead, I gulp half the glass in one go. "Leave the bottle," I tell her.

Aspen claps her hands. "The question-and-answer session will now begin." Everyone starts shouting out questions at once until Aspen whistles for quiet. "Raise your hand if you have a question and I'll call on you one by one."

"You sound like Mom," I grumble behind her. "Are you going to give out detention to those who don't listen?"

Mom sniffs. "I don't give out detention for students who don't listen." I widen my eyes at her obvious lie. "You got detention because you didn't follow directions, not because you didn't listen."

I'm not clear on the distinction she's making.

She crosses her arms over her chest. "I told you if you screamed 'I volunteer as tribute' one more time, I would give you detention."

"I don't understand why you got mad. I thought you'd be happy I was reading books. You're an English teacher after all."

She sniffs, and I raise my palm in her direction. "No. I don't want to hear how *The Hunger Games* isn't literature again. Let's agree to disagree."

"I'm still right," she sings as she finds a seat.

And people say I'm stubborn.

Aspen fists her hands on her hips. "Are you two finished?"

"I don't know. If I say I'm finished, are you going to let them," I motion to the crowd, "circle me like they're sharks and I'm bleeding from my foot?"

"Sharks don't go crazy when they smell blood. It's an urban myth," Juniper explains.

"Really?" I ask as if I'm fascinated. I'm not. I've been forced to watch enough Shark Weeks on the Discovery Channel to fulfill all my non-existent interest in sharks. I didn't learn anything other than swimming in the ocean is bad. I'll stick to pools, thank you very much.

"First question?" Aspen says and points to Feather. I groan. Feather doesn't know what a brain to filter is. Whatever pops into her brain shoots out of her mouth without any thought as to who her words might offend.

"Why porn?" Thanks for proving me right, Feather.

"Why porn what?" I ask in a delaying tactic I know will fail. At least, there's wine.

Unfortunately, Feather takes my question seriously. "Why do you narrate porn? Why not some other genre?"

I huff out a breath of air. "First of all, I do not narrate porn. I narrate erotic romance."

"What's the difference?"

"Erotic romance is a romance story, despite the explicit sex. In fact, the sex is not an inherent part of the story. You can remove it without damaging the storyline."

"Oh," Feather says and flops back into her seat.

"But why erotic romance? Why not thrillers or mysteries or romance without sex?" Petal asks.

"Are you saying you'd read a romance story without sex in it?" I fire back at her.

The questions continue in this line until I nearly finish the bottle of wine. I blame the wine for what happens next.

"Listen up." I clap my hands to get everyone's attention. "It's not some big secret why I narrate erotic romance."

"It's not? How disappointing," Clove mumbles.

I ignore her. "It's simple really. As everyone knows, I majored in drama at college. Interesting fact – tuition does not include costs for costumes unless you want to wear the costumes worn by a million students before you." My nose scrunches in disgust. "A professor mentioned something about narration as an opportunity to practice our acting skills while earning extra cash.

I signed up on this platform. Made an audition tape and waited. I was offered a gig to narrate an erotic romance and jumped at the chance to earn some cash. The reviewers went crazy over my 'raspy voice', which lead other erotic romance writers to seek me out. Things kind of snowballed from there. That's it. That's the story. I don't have some secret fetish for narrating erotic romance. I'm not a phone sex operator. It's my job. Plain and simple."

The door bangs open and Rowan stomps inside. He appears mad, and oh boy, does mad turn him from sexy to uber sexy. His lips, which I know from personal experience are soft, are turned down in a frown. He glares at me.

"What? I didn't do anything wrong." I lift my palms in a display of innocence and nearly fall off my chair. Oops. Didn't do anything wrong and drank an entire bottle of wine aren't the same thing, are they?

"Yes, they are when you should be home resting," Rowan responds.

Shit. Am I speaking my thoughts out loud? How much did I drink?

"A bottle and you should probably stop talking now," Moon answers.

I pretend to zip my lips and end up slumped to the side in my chair.

Rowan marches over to me and picks me up. I slap at his shoulders. "It's not time to go home yet, Jeeves."

"It is. You need your rest to help your bones heal."

He carries me toward the exit of the bookstore with no effort whatsoever and I know I'm not the lightest of women. Ha! I wish. My butt alone should have its own area code.

"Stop complaining, Ashlyn," Mom tells me. "I'd let a big, strong man like Rowan carry me around."

"I think Dad wouldn't be too happy about it."

Mom winks at me. "But he's sexy when he's jealous."

I groan. "Gross. Thanks, Mom. Now I have more material to discuss with my therapist."

"Why does she constantly refer to a therapist?" Lilac asks. "She's not actually in therapy."

Ellery pats her arm. "It's this thing we normal people refer to as sarcasm."

"I don't understand sarcasm."

"We know!" I shout together with Juniper.

Rowan grunts at her.

"He says 'if you're done bonding with Ash, could you please open the door?'," I explain.

"You can understand his grunts?" she asks, and Rowan grunts again.

"Uh oh. It's his impatient grunt."

She rushes to open the door. "Have a good night!"

As soon as the door shuts behind her, I shove Rowan's shoulders. "Put me down!"

I expect him to dump me on the back of his golf cart, but he doesn't. He lays me down with such gentleness my eyes water. Why does he have to be gentle with me and show me what I'm missing?

When we arrive at his house, I hop off the golf cart before he can stop me. He catches up to me on the way to his front door and lifts me into his arms again.

"Stop it! I'm not a child. Stop treating me like one."

He snorts. "I don't think you're a child, Ash."

My bottom lip juts out. "Whatever. Just take me to my room, Jeeves."

"You don't believe me?"

It doesn't matter if I believe him. I don't want to have this discussion.

He carries me into his house and down the hall to the bedroom I'm currently using. He lays me on the bed before kissing my forehead.

"I don't see you as a child, Ash. Quite the contrary," he whispers against my skin before leaving.

What the hell does he mean? Before I can begin to unravel the mystery of Rowan, the wine catches up to me and the world fades away.

Chapter 17

Slap-happy – a state of being dizzy with happiness, which is usually caused my multiple slaps to the head but can also be the result of losing crutches

I RUSH OUT OF the doctor's office – without my crutches – and spin around for the people in the waiting room, most of whom I don't know.

"I am free! I tell you – FREE!" I lift up my walking cast to show it off.

Juniper glares at me. "Please tell me you're not going to paint your face blue and pretend you're William Wallace."

"You have to admit Mel Gibson was pretty hot in *Braveheart*."

"So hot." She fans her face. "Although, the little ponytail he sported in *The Patriot* was dang sexy."

My sister is more crazy about movies than I am, which is saying a lot since I studied drama in college. I never imagined myself as a Hollywood star, though. Trust me, I know my ass is too big for those superficial Hollywood types. I don't actually know any Hollywood types, but I read *People* magazine.

"Come on," I grab her arm and drag her toward the exit of the doctor's office. "Let's go have lunch to celebrate."

"Aspen, Ellery, and Lilac are meeting us at the burger joint on the highway you're always raving about."

"Awesome!"

Since the only places to eat in Winter Falls are the diner and the brewery, I sometimes branch out to other locations to find some grub. Not as often as I'd wish. I don't own a car, after all. It's a good thing there are a few vehicles owned by the town, which residents are allowed to borrow for essential tasks. Unfortunately, 'dying for' a burger fix is not considered essential by the other residents of Winter Falls.

I prance into the burger joint showing off my walking cast to my sisters.

"Does this mean you're moving back in with Juniper?" Lilac asks, and I freeze on the spot in the middle of the restaurant.

How could I forget there's a time limit on my staying in Rowan's house? I knew living with him would be difficult. But I thought it would be difficult because of my unrequited love for him. I never imagined he'd kiss me and call me a mistake. Technically, he said the kiss was a mistake, but it felt like he was saying *I'm* the mistake.

But if I'm a mistake, why did he kiss my forehead? What the hell does 'quite the contrary' mean?

"Earth to Ashlyn." Juniper snaps her fingers in front of my face. "Where did you go?"

"I can imagine where she went." Aspen wiggles her eyebrows. "I think we all can after Rowan carried her out of the bookstore the other day like she's a damsel in distress and he's her knight in shining armor."

"Nothing happened," I'm quick to point out as I join them at their booth. And no way am I a damsel in distress.

Ellery gestures toward my face. "Your expression doesn't say nothing happened."

"Nothing happened the night of the book club."

"I surmise this to mean something happened on a different night." I glare at Lilac. "What? What did I do wrong now?"

Aspen claps. "I want to hear everything."

"Ew." Ellery feigns retching. "No. I don't want to hear the details of my sister's sexual exploits."

"Don't worry. There were no sexual exploits."

"But something happened. You can't deny it. You're as easy to read as an open book," Aspen claims.

"I'm hungry," I say instead of responding to her. I try to catch the eye of the waitress, but Aspen blocks me.

"No food until we get the details."

"What are you? The food police?" I stand, so I can see around her.

Juniper yanks me back down again. "You might as well tell us. We'll just keep pestering you until you do."

"I guess you don't want to hear about the latest development in the Mystery of the Black Hat Bandit's Missing Loot then."

"Aspen already told us," Ellery says.

"She did?" Lilac scans the faces of the rest of my sisters. "Nobody told me anything."

"First, sexy Rowan. After Ashlyn spills all her secrets, we'll talk mystery," Aspen declares.

"I want food first. The biggest, juiciest burger they have plus onion rings and maybe a shake."

"It's a good thing you can walk again. The meal you're describing is enough to meet your daily caloric intake requirements for two days."

I stick my tongue out at Lilac. How dare she remind me of calories?

"What? I'm merely stating a fact."

"Facts are boring."

She gasps. "Is this sarcasm? Please tell me this is sarcasm because facts are never boring. Facts are the very basis of our existence."

I stick my hand in her face before she can start to hyperventilate. Although, it's always fun to watch Lilac have human reactions. But I don't feel up to a return trip to the hospital when she becomes convinced she's having a heart attack because Lilac could never have a simple hissy fit.

"I was joking."

She clutches her chest as her breathing returns to normal. *You're mean* Juniper mouths to me, and I shrug. Isn't everyone a bit mean when it comes to their sisters? It's sibling law.

The waitress arrives and takes our orders. While she's scribbling away, I'm desperately trying to come up with a lie to tell my sisters about Rowan. I don't want them to know the man I've been in love with for-freaking-ever said I was a mistake. How embarrassing.

"Fess up," Aspen says as soon as the waitress is out of earshot.

Juniper rubs her hands together. "I want all the details."

Ellery feigns gagging again, but when I study her, I'm not convinced she's feigning anything. Her face is actually a bit green. Is she sick?

"Just tell us already," Lilac insists. "I want to get to the mystery part my sisters are apparently keeping from me."

"Fine. We kissed."

Aspen leans forward. "And? What happened next? Did he throw you over his shoulder and carry you into his bedroom before stripping you naked and having his wicked way with you?"

In my dreams. "Someone's been reading too many romance novels."

She gets this wistful expression on her face. "No need for romance novels. I have a real hero named Lyric." She waves her engagement ring in my face in case I forgot.

I haven't. It's hard to forget your sister being proposed to in front of the whole town. It was beyond romantic and I'm not the least bit jealous except for when I'm conscious.

"Well," Lilac prods when I don't add onto my story, "did you and Rowan have sexual intercourse?"

"Sexual intercourse? Way to make it sound romantic."

"It doesn't always have to be romantic. Sometimes sex is just sex," Ellery says.

Lilac nods. "I agree. Sex can be useful as a release and not be related to romance whatsoever."

Of course, my robot sister doesn't think sex is romantic. She also apparently has several men she can contact whenever she needs a 'release'. I try not to think too hard about it, because it's kind of sad.

I scan the table and notice all of my sisters are waiting for my response. I know those faces. They won't let me out of this place without telling them every last thing that happened.

Fine. I'll give in and tell them. "We kissed. Afterwards, he told me it was a mistake and left."

"What?" Aspen screeches. "What a jerk. We need to figure out a revenge plan. Ideas?"

"We could replace the sugar at the bakery with salt," Juniper suggests.

"Don't even think about it," Ellery moans. "He supplies the inn with baked goods for breakfast. I don't want to lose clients because the baker is an asshole who doesn't know a good thing when it's standing right in front of him."

I nearly thank her for sticking up for me, but I have a feeling she's no longer talking about Rowan and me.

"I can short out his electricity at his home," Lilac offers.

My mouth gapes open, and I stare at her.

"What? I am an engineer."

"Yeah. I know. I'm just surprised you'd use your powers for evil instead of good."

"I think getting revenge on an idiot is considered good."

I smile at her. "Thanks."

"You're my little sister. No one's allowed to mess with you."

"But I'm still living in the house with him, remember? Maybe we should put a pin in any revenge plans for now."

Aspen's nose wrinkles as she studies me. "Okay."

I nearly rear back at her response. Did my big sister actually agree with me? I think I need to note this in my diary. Except I don't keep a diary.

"Can we talk about the mystery now?" Lilac asks as the waitress arrives with our food.

Once the waitress leaves, I survey the restaurant to make certain no one is paying any attention to us. Everyone looks busy with their food, but I lean forward and whisper just in case.

"Aspen and I went to the brewery, and we discovered an old safe there."

"How old?" Lilac asks.

"Let me finish," I shush her. "Anyway, in the safe was a sealed letter from Robert to Patricia, as in the black hat bandit to his lover. Apparently, Robert wrote the letter in case he wasn't around when Patricia arrived in town. In it he says, and I quote here, 'you'll find the item referred to in the temporary tablecloth'. The item referred to is obviously the loot from the bank robbery."

"But what about the temporary tablecloth? What does that mean?" Lilac asks.

Aspen bounces in her seat. "It's a clue."

Lilac rolls her eyes. "Yes, I understand it's a clue. But what does the clue mean?"

Aspen shrugs and now it's my turn to bounce in my seat because I think I've figured the clue out.

"You don't know?" I ask and bat my lashes in a bid to appear innocent.

Aspen's eyes widen. "You figured out the clue?" I nod. "Come on. Tell us."

"What can be used as a temporary tablecloth?"

"A blanket? A sheet?"

"Nope," I say making sure to pop the P. Thanks to my stupid broken ankle, I've had plenty of time to do crossword puzzles. Once I thought of the clue as a crossword clue, I didn't need much time to figure it out.

"No other guesses?" When everyone merely stares in response, I declare, "It's a newspaper."

"What newspaper could it be? The *Winter Falls Post* didn't begin printing until 1960, but the robbery occurred in 1955." Lilac reminds me of the facts I already know.

"I don't know, but I'm convinced I'm right about the clue. I'll do some research and figure it out."

Heaven knows I need something to occupy my mind instead of obsessing about what Rowan meant when he kissed my forehead the other night. He had to kiss me and whisper against my forehead like I was precious. I'm a mistake. Not precious.

Chapter 18

Score an own goal – when you think you scored for the opposition, but you really scored for yourself

"What the hell?"

I jolt upright in bed at the shout. I rub my eyes and scan the room to try and figure out what's going on, but there's no one in my room. It must be Rowan shouting somewhere else in the house, but why? What happened? I hear more cursing. Someone's angry.

Sigh. Guess I better go figure out what's going on. I follow the sound of cursing to the guest bedroom where Rowan is currently sleeping. I knock but enter before he can respond.

"Why are you—" My question screeches to a halt when I notice why he's pissed. "Damn Aspen. I'm going to kill her."

Rowan jolts. "What are you doing in here? And where are your crutches?"

"Ta da!" I lift my walking cast. "I got this fashion accessory today. All the cool kids have one."

Something he'd know if we weren't avoiding each other. I thought I was the queen of avoidance, but Rowan's better at it. Since the forehead kiss, I can't stop thinking about, I've barely seen him. I don't know where he's hanging out in the evenings, but it's not in his house in front of his television where he can usually be found.

"Great." He pauses and I wonder if he's going to tell me to go home since I'm now mobile. "But I don't want you climbing too many stairs. A walking cast is still a cast."

Relief hits me at his words and its force nearly knocks me to the floor. I didn't realize how much I feared he was going to tell me to go home until this very minute.

"What's going on here?" I ask and motion to the spot where his bed should be before I can do something incredibly stupid such as tell him I never want to leave.

"You tell me."

I rear back. "What? You think I did this. How the hell did I manage it on one foot?"

"If anyone could, it's you."

My chest puffs out. "True. But I have no idea who stole your bed."

He raises an eyebrow and crosses his arms over his chest. My gaze drops to watch how his bicep muscles flex with the motion. I bite my lip to stop myself from licking it or, you know, licking any part of his body.

He clears his throat and I realize I've been staring at his muscles longer than is polite, although no one's ever accused me of being polite before.

"What? I'm not lying."

"You've been home all evening and you didn't hear a thing?"

I fist my hands at my hips. "No, Mr. Accuser, I did not. I worked all evening on a new assignment." When he continues to stare at me, I explain. "I was in the closet with my headphones on. The house could have burned down around me, and I wouldn't have heard."

He frowns and mumbles something about a security system underneath his breath. I don't ask him to clarify. Not when he's acting all big brother again.

"I guess I'll sleep on the couch."

"Don't be stupid. You can sleep in your bed."

"I am not letting you sleep on the couch with a broken ankle."

I roll my eyes. "I'm not sleeping on the couch. We can share a bed. It's no big deal. The bed is practically the size of Rhode Island anyway. I'll stick to my side. You can stick to yours."

I really hope I can stick to my side. Who knows what my lustful body will do once I'm asleep? But I can't let him sleep on the sofa. It's too short for him and he needs to work in the morning.

"Come on." I motion for him to follow me as I hobble toward the main bedroom I've been staying in. "I promise not to maul you in the middle of the night." At least, not consciously.

I climb back into bed and settle into what is now my side of the bed. I don't cling to the edge. There's no need. I wasn't joking about how big this bed is. The lights switch off before the bed dips to indicate Rowan has joined me.

"Good night." I do my best to sound normal despite feeling as if my body just lit up from being jolted by a thousand tasers. Actually, a taser would probably have less effect on me than the man laying next to me.

"Good night," he grunts.

I'm certain I won't fall asleep anytime soon. Not with the object of my infatuation laying in the same bed as me. But I close my eyes and the exhaustion of the day hits me and I'm out.

I moan as I come awake. Wow. That feels good. This is a damn good dream. A large hand kneads my breast as another hand splays over my stomach. I grind my ass into the body behind me and feel his hard length push against me.

Whoa. This isn't a dream. This is real. This is Rowan's hand touching me, making me wet, making me want to beg for more.

I'm not one to question good fortune. I'll probably regret this in the morning when he says I'm a mistake again, but I'm grabbing my slice of heaven right now.

I reach behind me and wrap an arm around his head. His lips find my neck and he begins placing open mouthed kisses there. Goosebumps break out across my skin, and I arch to give him better access. He licks and nips at the area until he reaches my ear. There, he bites the lobe and I moan before turning my head so my lips can meet his.

He nibbles on my lower lip, and I gasp at how good the sting of his teeth feels. He uses the opportunity to thrust his tongue into my mouth. My tongue rushes to meet his. Our tongues duel as his hand on my breast becomes more aggressive.

When he pinches my nipple, I groan and lose his mouth when my head falls back against his chest. He continues to torture my nipple with one hand while his other hand travels from my stomach down my front until he hits my panties.

His hand sneaks underneath the material and finds my seam where he brushes his finger up and down. It feels good, but it's not enough. I throw my leg over his opening myself up to him.

"Good girl," he mumbles.

If I could speak, I'd tell him I'm not a good girl. But the ability to talk leaves me when his finger finds my clit. He rubs circles around it until I'm grinding my core into his hand, silently begging for more. He doesn't disappoint. His hand moves lower until he finds my center. He thrusts into me, and I groan from how freaking wonderful his thick finger invading my body feels.

This is better than anything I could have imagined in my dreams. And, trust me, it felt pretty damn good in my dreams. I have an excellent imagination.

"Ride my hand, Ash."

Yes. Oh god. Yes. He remembers who I am. He's not merely dreaming or taking advantage of having a willing woman in his bed. It's me and he knows it.

My arm around his neck tightens as I follow his instruction and ride his hand. My other hand moves to my neglected breast, and I play with my nipple.

"Holy fuck, that's hot."

"Hell yeah, it is," I croak, surprised I still know how to use words with everything my body is feeling.

Each time he plucks at my nipple, my walls tighten around his finger, and I become even wetter. He adds another finger and goodness gracious does it feel good to be full of him.

Tingles spread from my stomach and my entire body heats as my climax barrels down on me.

"I'm going to—"

Before I can finish the words, I jump off the cliff into a pool of pleasure. I hear moaning and realize it must be me. I'm not embarrassed, though. I'm too busy enjoying the ride to care about what sounds I'm making.

I ride out my orgasm until my body is spent and I collapse against the heat of Rowan's body. I can feel his cock hot and hard against my ass. I reach down to squeeze him.

"Ash, don't."

"Why not?"

"If you keep squeezing me, I won't be able to stop myself from having you, and I don't have a condom."

"Not a problem. I'm on birth control and I'm clean."

He moans as I twist my wrist and squeeze him. "You're sure?"

I've never been more sure of anything in my life. This is my every sexual fantasy come true.

"Yes," I hiss.

He grasps my wrist and places my hand back around his neck before pulling down his boxers. My panties are shoved to the side before he places his cock at my entrance.

"You ready for this?"

I squirm in response to his deep, growly voice. "I've been ready."

He thrusts inside me and my back arches with how good it feels to be filled by him. He's thick and wide, and I can feel him everywhere.

He slowly retreats and I clench my inner muscles to keep him where I want him.

Rowan growls before punching his hips and thrusting inside me again. "You asked for it," he grunts.

Hell yeah, I did.

I hold on for the ride as he finds his rhythm. With every thrust he makes, I push back into him. The room is filled with the sound of skin slapping against skin and my moans. The noise serves to spur on my excitement more.

"Not gonna last long. Need you to come," he grumbles before his hand snakes between us to find my clit.

"Come for me, Ash. For me."

He rubs my clit as his thrusts speed up and I'm a goner. My nails dig into his neck as my climax rushes through my body.

"Rowan," I groan as my body clenches around him.

His thrusts become erratic and his breath hitches.

"Ash. Ash. Ash," he recites as I feel him fill me with his seed. His fingers on my breast squeeze until I'm sure I'll have bruises there tomorrow. I don't care. I'll proudly wear them as a reminder.

He buries his face in my hair as his front collapses against my back. His hand drops from my breast to band around my waist.

"Sleep, my dream. Sleep."

My body sated, I have no problem following his order and fall into a deep, dreamless sleep.

Chapter 19

Sideline – to be removed from participation by an unexpected guest

I SMILE AS I stretch and slowly come awake. I haven't felt this good in the morning since— I freeze for a moment before forcing myself to evaluate my body. Yep. I'm sore in areas I haven't been sore in since the last time I had sex. Sex. Holy donuts in the sky – I had sex with Rowan last night.

And it was better than I could have ever imagined. I know sex can feel good. You don't grow up with my mom without knowing about sex and how good it can make you feel as well as how many types of contraception there are and which ones are the most dependable. But dear chocolate goddesses in the heavens, I did not know sex could feel *this* good.

I reach behind me for Rowan, but the sheets are cold. I check the clock and notice it's nearly nine. He must be at the bakery by now. After all, his business doesn't grind to a halt just because the owner had an amazing night of sex. Hold on. Did Rowan think the sex was amazing, too?

Nope! *Stop it, Ash.* You are not going to spend the morning evaluating and analyzing every single thing he said and sound he made. You are going to get out of this bed, tame your sex hair – although maybe take a selfie for future reference – and get to work.

I nod to myself before throwing the covers off and marching to the bathroom.

Several hours later, I remove my headphones and switch off my microphone. I can't believe it. I nearly finished my new assignment today. Granted, the erotica I'm narrating is a novella, but still. I flew through the pages like nobody's business. Except everyone was getting the business in this story. Every-freaking-one.

Phew. I stand and stretch my back. It's sore from sitting in the same position for the past – I check the clock – three hours. No wonder my muscles are screaming at me.

Bang! Bang!

I whip my head around at the sound. Is there someone at the door? I grab my phone off the make-up desk in the walk-in closet and notice it's half past noon. Maybe one of my sisters is stopping by with some grub. Awesome. My stomach rumbles in agreement.

I make my way to the front door and open it. Except it doesn't open. Is it locked? Since when do people in Winter Falls lock their doors? I roll my eyes. Rowan must think he can keep my sisters from pulling pranks on him by locking the door. Silly man. Doesn't he know my family better by now?

I unlock the door and unlatch the security cable before opening it. My pleasant greeting gets caught in my throat when I notice who's standing on the porch. I wish I could say

I don't know who she is, but I'd be lying. Of course, I know who Sandra Hansley is. Rowan's ex-wife.

"Can I help you?"

She tries to plow past me, but I'm no pushover – walking cast or not. I cross my arms over my chest and block her.

"I asked if I can help you," I repeat between grit teeth.

There is exactly one person on the entire earth who can ruin my happiness this morning and I'm staring at her. I consider lifting my boot and kicking her off the porch, but I don't know what Rowan would think of my actions. Does he still love her? The online articles about their divorce were scant on the details.

"Where's Rowan?"

I cock a brow. "Where's Rowan?" If she knew anything at all about her ex-husband, she'd know exactly where to find him.

"I didn't stutter. Answer my question."

I study the woman standing in front of me. The woman who had everything I ever desired and threw it all away. What kind of fool is she? I can't deny she's a gorgeous fool. Her brunette hair frames her face in perfect wisps. She has bright green eyes and a lush mouth.

And the perfection doesn't stop there. Of course not. Her perfect face tops a perfect body. She's tall and thin, and I'm sure if she turns around, she won't have a bubble butt like I do. To complete the comparison I'm obviously losing, her breasts fill out her bra nicely creating a wealth of cleavage whereas I rarely bother to wear a bra at all.

I answer her question with a question of my own. "Why don't you message him and find out?"

She frowns or at least I assume she's frowning, her face doesn't have much expression. How much Botox do you have to inject into your body before you lose the ability to make facial expressions?

"His phone must be switched off."

I shrug. "Then, call his business."

Her nose scrunches as if she smells something rotten. "The bakery?"

I roll my eyes. "Yeah, the bakery."

"Why would my husband be at the bakery?"

"He's not your husband," someone hollers from the front lawn.

Sandra startles before she whips around to glare at whoever spoke. I use the movement to my advantage and push her out of the doorway. I follow her out and shut the door behind us.

"What did you say?" she screeches.

I scan the lawn and notice we've got ourselves a crowd. Feather, Petal, Sage, Cayenne, and Clove are all standing there with their arms crossed over their chests. I'm surprised they don't have pitchforks in their hands. Although, where would they find pitchforks in a hurry?

"I said," Cayenne speaks slowly and enunciates her words, "he is not your husband."

Sandra waves away her comment. "Husband, ex-husband, it's all the same."

"Um, no. It's not," I tell her.

She lifts an eyebrow and appraises me. "Don't delude yourself into thinking you can make Rowan happy, my dear. I admit your country bumpkin outfit does have some charm, but I'm sure your relationship with my husband will be fleeting."

Before I have a chance to ask her who she thinks she is, Sage speaks, "Because you're the expert? How long were you married before he dumped you?"

Sandra snorts. "Rowan didn't dump me. I don't get dumped."

Naturally. Ms. Perfect Face and Body would never get dumped.

"Only because you dump a man before he can dump you," Clove says. The other women must agree since they high-five each other.

"I kindly ask you to keep your nose out of my business," Sandra says primly.

"Lady, you made your divorce the world's business when you tattled to the gossip columns. How much money did you earn for tattling anyway? Is telling secrets to the tabloids how you earn your money now?" Petal asks and thus begins another round of high-fives.

I clap my hands. "Ladies, ladies, why don't you return to … whatever you were doing before you came here, and I'll accompany Sandra to the bakery?"

Feather snorts. "We're not going anywhere. Besides, Rowan will be here any minute."

Great. This is exactly how I wanted to encounter Rowan the morning after the first time we have sex. He's going to be reminded of everything Sandra is and everything I'm not. He won't need any time at all to figure out he's out of my league.

"Don't you have a business to manage?" I ask Feather before my thoughts can spiral any further.

She grins. "Lunch break."

"You run an ice cream shop. Lunch break is your rush hour." Trust me, I know. I've spent enough lunch hours trying to handle the mass of tourists demanding a scoop of homemade frozen delight.

"It's the middle of the week and tourist season is over."

Dang it. She's not wrong. I turn to Sage. Surely, she needs to get back to the police station.

"I'm on my lunch break," she says before I can speak. "Stop trying to get us to leave. It's not going to happen."

I sigh. I don't know why I bothered. "Whatever," I mutter before returning to the problem I can deal with. I hope.

"Let me grab my purse and I'll walk you over to the bakery."

"Sorry, Ashlyn, I can't let you walk to the bakery," Cayenne says. "Rowan will kill us if he knows we let you walk that far."

"Far? From what I've seen, this town is tiny. I'm sure she can walk the block needed."

From what she's seen? Hasn't Sandra been here before? Winter Falls is Rowan's hometown. They were married. Didn't he bring her home to meet his parents? Granted his parents are now retired and live in Florida in a house Rowan bought for them, but they only relocated two years ago after Rowan was forced to retire early from the NFL. Sandra and Rowan were married until two years ago.

"She has a broken ankle," Cayenne explains.

Sandra glances down at my feet. She must notice the boot on my foot. It's hard to miss after all. She looks around before noticing the golf cart. "We can use the cart."

"You are not going anywhere with Ash," Rowan growls as he rushes to the porch.

How did I miss his approach? Oh yeah, I was preoccupied by Ms. Sunshine here.

I glance around the lawn and notice Aspen has arrived as well. She waves at me and gives me a thumbs-up. Why is she giving me a thumbs-up? This is a disaster.

"Show's over!" Rowan glares at the crowd on the lawn. Does he seriously expect them to give up and leave? Not likely.

"I'll just …" I wave toward the inside of the house and retreat before either one of them has a chance to stop me.

I move as fast as my boot will allow to the bedroom. I stare at the messed up sheets on the bed where I made love to Rowan last night. I hope I committed every single detail to memory since it was probably the first and last time I'll have him in my bed.

I shut myself in the bedroom and turn on the fan before I succumb to my tears.

Chapter 20

Run interference – to handle someone else's problems by solving your own dang problems

ROWAN

I whistle as I pour the cupcake dough into the tray. I usually struggle to wake up and get to the bakery on time but not this morning. Today I can accomplish anything I put my mind to. Maybe I'll try a new recipe out this morning.

"What are you happy about?" Bryan asks as he strolls into the kitchen of the bakery.

"Does there have to be a reason?"

He gasps. "You're answering a question with a question, which means you're hiding information from me." He pauses to peruse my face. "Oh my word! You slept with Ashlyn. It's about time!"

I put the tray of cupcakes in the oven before whirling around to confront him. "We are not discussing this."

He claps. "Yeah! It's serious. It's about time you got over your bitch of an ex-wife. Ashlyn is the perfect rebound girl."

I growl. "Ash is no one's rebound girl."

He squeals. "It is serious! I knew it! Finally, it's my turn to win the bet. It's about time. I've been here two years now and I haven't won a single bet yet."

My hands are around his throat before I realize I'm moving. "Ash and I aren't a joking matter." I drop my hand. "Ash and I aren't a couple anyway."

He rolls his eyes. "Sure, you aren't, Mr. Hot and Cold. You care for her more than you're willing to admit. It's time you got over She Who Shall Not Be Named and moved on with your life. You deserve to be happy."

I don't deserve to be happy unless I can make my woman happy and I can't, which means I don't deserve love.

Bryan sighs. "You've retreated into your big silent man persona once again. I'll go get the front of the house ready to open." He stomps away but stops with his hand on the door and glances back at me over his shoulder. "Have you ever considered you couldn't make Sandra happy because no one can make her happy?"

I motion for him to get going. I don't want to discuss my ex-wife with him. He's the one person who was with me through it all. He knows everything Sandra said and did. Well, not everything. There's one thing no one else knows. My secret shame.

"You know I'm right," he sings as he sashays away.

Easy for him to say. He doesn't realize I couldn't give Sandra the one thing she wanted.

An hour later, with a tray of cupcakes in my arms, I elbow the door to the bakery open. As soon as I step into the room, silence falls. I frown as I scan the crowd. Everyone is staring at me as if they're evaluating me.

I know these stares. I became accustomed to them when I played ball. They're definitely evaluating me, but now it's not about how many yards I can throw for a touchdown. No, the good people of Winter Falls are wondering what my romantic future entails.

I should have expected this. You can't keep a secret in this town and Ash has made no attempt to keep her feelings about me private since she returned home last year after graduating college. But I never imagined everyone would know I'd slept with her within hours. We haven't even had the morning after talk yet!

Aspen comes rushing into the bakery. "I'm not discussing my sex life with your sister with you," I tell her before she can speak.

Applause erupts from the crowd and money exchanges hands. Bryan slaps me on the back. "My vacation piggy bank thanks you."

I drop my chin and rub my neck. Damnit. This town drives me crazy sometimes.

"I need your help," Aspen shouts to be heard above the crowd.

My legs eat up the space between us. "What is it? What's wrong? Is Ash hurt? She better not be walking around. She's still in a cast whether she thinks she is or not."

She leans close to whisper, "Sandra's here."

"What did you say, lassie? I didn't hear you," Basil, the hippie headbanger tow truck driver, yells.

I ignore him and everyone else. Sandra's here? In Winter Falls? She refused to visit my parents in town when we were married. What the hell is she doing here now?

I plow through the crowd. Once I'm outside, I sprint toward my house. I wish I had my golf cart, but I only use it when it's raining, or I have a load of groceries to carry.

What the hell is Sandra saying to Ash? Fuck. Is she going to ruin everything? Wait. Is there anything to ruin? I force those thoughts out of my mind. Now is not the time to worry about my relationship with Ash.

When I reach the house, Sandra is staring Ash down. She motions to the golf cart and practically orders Ash to bring her to me. Princess Sandra strikes again.

"You are not going anywhere with Ash," I growl when I reach the porch.

"Show's over!" I glower at the crowd on the lawn until they give up and begin dispersing.

"I'll just …" Ash waves toward the inside the house and retreats before I have a chance to stop her. I'll deal with her later. The bigger problem is standing right in front of me.

"Rowan," Sandra purrs as she drags a sharp fingernail down my chest.

I capture her hand. I don't want her hands on me. There's only one woman whose hands I want to feel on my body, and she just ran away looking like I destroyed her microphone and stomped on her laptop. Fuck!

"You don't touch me," I growl at her.

"You tell her, Rowan!" The crowd cheers.

Shit. I thought I got rid of our spectators. But when I turn my glare on them, they shrug and shuffle their feet. They're not going anywhere. Fine. If they won't leave, I will.

I open the door to my house and drag Sandra inside. I don't want her in my house – the home I've been sharing with Ash for the past weeks – but what choice do I have?

"What do you want?"

"I want you back, of course. Why else would I be in this honky-tonk town?" She tilts her chin up as if she's better than everyone in this town. Not hardly.

I cross my arms over my chest. "What makes you think I would take you back?"

"Darling, we both know I'm the only woman who will accept your little problem."

Little problem? How dare she bring up my problem? Wait. Shit. Did she tell Ash? Is that why she ran away as soon as I arrived? Does she realize I'm damaged goods now? I want to follow her, but I need to get rid of my ex first.

"What's wrong?" I sneer. "Did you use up all of my money?"

Her gaze drops to the floor. Bingo!

"I'm not a football player in the NFL anymore, Sandra. I don't have millions to give you."

She glances around my house. "You're not hurting for cash."

Because I'm smart and invested my money. Or at least what money was left over after I was forced to hand over half of my earnings to her in our divorce. I'm the one who sweat and bled for that money. She's the one who spent it all on purses and shoes. The judge didn't care, though. How is fifty/fifty fair when one partner worked and the other used shopping as an excuse to day drink?

"And you have your business."

My heart spasms as if she reached inside my chest cavity and squeezed my heart. I force myself to take a breath. I made damn sure the money I used when I established the bakery was free and clear of Sandra. She can't get her grubby fingers on it.

I snort. "And how much money do you think a bakery in a – what did you call it again? – a honky-tonk town earns?"

Thanks to the tourists in the summer, I make a more than decent living, but nothing Sandra would accept. If she can't buy a new thousand-dollar handbag each and every day, it's not enough money. Her priorities are seriously whacked.

"I know the bakery is merely a consolation prize after what happened."

"What happened?" I grumble. "You mean my knee being crushed and having to learn how to walk again?"

And Sandra, being the caring wife she was, left me while I was still struggling with my recovery. The doctors said there was no way I could play professional football again and she couldn't get out the door fast enough. Bryan's not wrong when he says my ex's a bitch.

She looks me up and down. "Let's leave the past in the past, shall we? You're walking now, aren't you?"

Thanks to hours and hours of grueling physical therapy, sleepless nights when the pain nearly undid me, and more ice baths than any man should have to endure. I thought my balls were going to permanently lodge themselves in my scrotum when I continued to freeze them off in ice bath after ice bath.

"You do realize I'll never play football again, don't you? I'll never earn the millions you need to live in the style you've become accustomed to."

Those are the exact words the judge used. I had to give up half of my income because Sandra had the right to lead her life 'in the style she'd become accustomed to'. What a crock of shit.

She crosses her arms over her chest, pushing up her breasts. She's not stupid. She knows the action used to drive me wild. Good thing I'm no longer led around by my dick. Besides, I know how real breasts feel in my hands now. I won't settle for fake any longer.

"Let me make this clear for you. This," I wave my hand between the two of us, "is never going to happen. I'm never going to take you back."

She shakes her head at me like I'm a little boy who doesn't know his own mind. "Why must you drag this out?"

"Are you on crack? I'm not dragging anything out. We are done. The divorce papers are signed. You've had your settlement money. There's nothing for us to discuss."

"Where shall I sleep in the meantime? I assume you have a guest room in this house," she says as if she didn't hear a thing I've been saying for the past fifteen minutes.

I'm done with this. I clamp my hand around her upper arm and drag her to the front door. It opens before I can reach it.

"Hi!" Aspen waves. "We're here to pick up our sister."

She doesn't bother to wait for my response before she presses past me with her sisters trailing after her. Ellery ignores me while Lilac gives me a tight smile and Juniper narrows her eyes on me.

"Who are these creatures?" Sandra asks.

I don't bother answering her. She's not part of my life anymore.

I lead her outside and notice her luggage on my porch. What the hell? Was she planning on moving in with me?

"Have a nice life," I tell her as I return to my front door.

"But where will I go?"

Shit. As much as I'd enjoy throwing her out, I can't. I can't be a complete asshole to the woman I used to love. Although, considering the way I feel for Ash, I can't help but wonder if what I felt for Sandra was ever love.

I turn around and pick up her luggage. Her frown changes into a smirk.

"Come on," I say as I march to my golf cart. "There's a lovely bed and breakfast in town."

"But—"

"You coming or not," I demand, but I don't wait for her response.

Chapter 21

Round – a phase of competition put into motion by a bunch of nosy sisters

THE BATHROOM DOOR flies open, and I jump to my feet before whirling around to confront Rowan. My shoulders fall when I realize he's not here. It's my sisters. I should have known. Rowan's too busy dealing with his *wife* to worry about me.

"The door was locked," I snarl.

Aspen snorts. "As if a locked door can keep us out."

True. I do know better.

"Why are you hiding in the bathroom?" Lilac asks as she studies the room. "Although it is a lovely bathroom."

"This bathtub is big enough for me and Bark Twain and Indiana Bones." Juniper climbs straight into the soaking tub, clothes and all. She sighs as she gets all comfy. "I could live in here."

"Personally, I love how the toilet is in a separate room. Helps with smells if you know what I mean." Ellery's nose bunches up as she nods to the toilet room.

Aspen plants her hands on her hips. "Can we get to the matter at hand or does everyone need more time to evaluate Rowan's bathroom?"

"I need more time," Lilac shouts from the toilet room. "There's a Japanese toilet in here." She shuts the door. "Don't mind me. I've always wanted to try one of these."

"Is she peeing?" Juniper asks from her position in the bathtub. "I can't hear it and I'm practically sitting next to her. How cool!"

"Why were you on the floor crying?" Ellery asks from the shower. "If you're going to cry in the bathroom, you might as well enjoy six jets of pulsating water." She caresses the jets as if she's touching a lover.

"Are you finished now?" Aspen yells.

The toilet flushes and Lilac appears. "I'm done, and I highly recommend the toilet. No need for a BOB with that toilet." She looks pointedly at Ellery who snorts in response.

"Trust me. BOB is gathering dust in my bedside table."

"Really? Why?" Juniper asks. "You couldn't gush enough about him at last month's book club."

"It's like herding cats," Aspen mumbles under her breath before clearing her throat. "We're not here to evaluate Rowan's bathroom."

"Maybe not. But I rate this bathtub a five out of five. Highly recommend." Juniper gives a thumbs-up.

"Get out of there!" Aspen orders. "We're here to cheer Ashlyn up since Rowan's wife showed up."

"Why?" Lilac frowns. "Ashlyn and Rowan aren't involved. The arrival of Rowan's *ex*-wife shouldn't affect her."

"Beep! Wrong!" Juniper indicates my face with a sweep of her hand. "She's been crying in the bathroom."

Ellery rolls her eyes. "Of course, she has. She's been pining away for Rowan forever. Even if the two aren't involved, being confronted with his former wife will be emotional for her."

Aren't involved? Are we not involved? We had sex. When I have sex with a man, I'm involved. Was last night a one night stand kind of thing for Rowan? Shit. I should have never let him sleep in the same bed as me. I knew I was asking for trouble, but I did it anyway. At some point in my life, I'm going to learn to walk away from trouble. Too bad that point wasn't last night.

"Ashlyn's being awful quiet." Aspen taps her chin as she contemplates me.

"What? What are you looking at?" I don't still have sex hair, do I? I pat at my hair.

Juniper rolls out of the bathtub and rushes to me. "I know this face." She squishes my cheeks between her hands. "Ashlyn had sex!"

"Can you keep it down? Ms. Perfect doesn't need to know I slept with her husband."

She releases me to punch a fist in the air. "Yes! I win the bet." She dances around the bathroom while humming the Rocky theme. Unfortunately, the bathroom is actually large enough for her to dance around in despite there being five of us in here so there's nothing to stop her.

"Keep it down!" I yell at her.

"You don't need to worry. Rowan was kicking her out when we arrived," Aspen informs me.

"He was?" I clear my throat to rid myself of the hope in my voice. "Doesn't matter. You should lower the volume, so Rowan can't hear you. Our business is our business."

Aspen barks out a laugh. "What delusional world do you live in? This is Winter Falls. Everyone at the bakery already figured out Rowan had sex with you."

My eyes widen. "You're kidding me."

"Nope. When I arrived there to tell Rowan his ex was bothering you, the news about his sexcapades was already spreading."

I bury my face in my hands. "Sexcapades?"

Good grief. Did Rowan tell everyone what we did last night? No, I refuse to believe it. He's not the kind of guy to kiss and tell. I'm positive since I've spent the past year trying to figure out why his marriage failed, and no one was talking.

"Yeah," Aspen says and hops onto the vanity. She brushes her hand over the marble. "This is nice."

"Can everyone stop loving on the bathroom?" I screech.

"Uh oh. She's about to blow. We need Long Island Iced Teas and chicken wings. Stat." Juniper shackles my wrist and tugs me toward the door.

I refuse to move my booted foot causing Juniper to stumble to a halt. "Are you kidding me? I'm not going out there!"

I was worried enough about the morning after talk and now I've got to deal with the ex talk on the same day. No thanks. Call me a chicken. No, I'm more of an ostrich. I'll bury my head in the sand and suffocate to death rather than deal with this whole mess.

"No worries. We'll use the window in the guest bedroom. The screen is still off of it."

I glare at Aspen. "You're the one who removed the bed from the guest bedroom." It's not a question.

She bows. "You're welcome."

Does she think I'll be thanking her? Not in this lifetime.

"How dare you?"

"I warned you when you wouldn't stop bugging me about Lyric, I'd get my revenge." She lifts her arms in the air and twirls around. "Welcome to my revenge."

"You can take revenge on me anytime, Aspen. I can deal with a little annoyance for that bathtub."

I raise an eyebrow at Juniper. She is such a liar. She has her own little annoyance she's been avoiding for years. A bathtub wouldn't be enough payment for her.

Lilac consults her watch. "Are we going to have lunch anytime soon? I have a meeting at four."

Ellery threads her arm through Lilac's. "You better cancel it. Unless you can handle a business meeting after drinking Long Island Ice Teas."

Lilac sniffs. "I don't drink Long Island Ice Teas."

"You do today," Ellery sings before dragging her to the door and marching out.

"Wait! I told you I'm not going out there."

"You can't hide in this bathroom forever," Juniper says with a wistful glance toward the tub.

"I can try," I mumble, but my sisters ignore me. Naturally.

Aspen and Juniper each secure an arm and drag me out of the bathroom and down the hallway to the guest bedroom.

"Where's the bed anyway?" I ask as I notice the empty space in the middle of the room where the bed used to be.

"Plausible deniability," Aspen says.

"I guess her living with a cop won't be so bad after all," Juniper whispers-shouts to me.

Personally, I never worried about Aspen being engaged to the Chief of Police. Lyric doesn't harass me for my little stunts as long as no one gets injured – too badly – and property isn't destroyed. Otherwise, what's the harm in a little fun?

Ellery shoves the windowsill up but pauses and shakes her head while backing away. "I'll go around to the front door and make sure the coast is clear." She rushes off before anyone can call her a chicken.

Lilac stares after her for a while before finally shrugging her shoulders. "I guess you expect me to jump through the window."

"I don't expect anything. I was perfectly happy in the bathroom," I mutter, but she's already out the window.

"Long Island Iced Teas," Juniper sings. "Chicken wings."

"Add chocolate to the mix and I promise to stop complaining for fifteen minutes."

"Thirty," she bargains.

We shake on it before she sweeps her arm toward the window. Yeah. Yeah. I get the hint already.

I dive through it headfirst and roll in the lawn before coming to stop next to Lilac who's brushing imaginary dust off her suit pants.

"The coast is clear," Ellery announces as she rushes toward us from the front door.

"Let's move," I say and begin marching toward *Electric Vibes.*

If ever there was an excuse to day drink, being confronted with your roommate's ex-wife the day after you accidentally slept with said roommate, is it.

A golf cart rolls to a stop next to me. "Hop in," Mom says.

I don't hesitate to listen to her since my ankle is already killing me. Standing while having a meet and greet with a bitchy woman will do that to a girl. And, okay, maybe I shouldn't have dove headfirst out of a window. In my defense, I let my shoulder take the brunt of the fall. It's not my first time using a window as an escape route after all.

"Where to?" Mom asks once my sisters have piled into the golf cart.

"Do you need to ask?"

"*Feather's Frozen Delights* it is," she says and takes a left turn.

Ice cream? Has she lost her mind? "Please tell me you're kidding."

She barks out a laugh. "Of course, I am." She pats my hand. "My baby wants her Long Island Iced Teas and chicken wings."

Geez. Am I this predictable?

Mom winks over at me. "A mother knows all." I hope not all. "All," she repeats.

My cheeks warm up and I glance away. She doesn't let me escape, though. Not my mom who thinks sex education should start at the age of six.

"There's nothing to be embarrassed about. You and Rowan are adults. You're both single and not involved with other people. You're allowed to enjoy yourselves as long as you're careful about prophylactics."

"Whatever you say, Mom," I mumble to cover up my gasp as I remember how I told Rowan a condom wasn't necessary last night. And here I thought I couldn't be a bigger idiot than I already am. And the biggest dunce award goes to …. Me!

Chapter 22

Roll with the punches – to take adversity in stride instead of punching aforementioned adversity in the face

ROWAN

I throw Sandra's suitcases into the golf cart, and she gasps. I knew throwing her designer luggage would rile her up. Ask me if I care.

"Save it," I tell her as I jump in. "Get in."

She huffs but does as I say. Maybe she's not as stupid as she acts.

"I—"

And maybe I spoke too soon.

"Stop. I don't want to hear whatever you're going to say. You left me. You divorced me. Why the hell would I want you back?"

She leans back in her seat to cross her legs. "You used not to be able to get enough of me," she says as she bobs her ankle.

Does she think her thousand-dollar Louboutin's are going to influence me? No thanks. The fact I even know what those shoes are called and how much they cost annoys any interest straight out of me. I much prefer a girl who runs around barefooted half the time.

My hands tighten on the steering wheel until my knuckles whiten. I should have left Sandra standing on my front porch with her expensive luggage and impractical shoes.

"This town has a certain…ahem… charm to it I guess," she says as we drive down Main Street toward *The Inn on Main*. I hope someone's there to check Sandra in since the owner, Ellery, just invaded my house to comfort Ash.

Ash. I rub a hand over my chest where it begins to ache. She must be furious with me. First, I left the bed this morning after making love to her in the middle of the night without saying a word. I should have at least left a note, but I barely made it out of the door in time to begin baking. I was too preoccupied with staring down at her blonde hair feathered over my pillows. As if leaving the house after not saying a word weren't enough, my ex-wife shows up and harasses her.

I stop the golf cart in front of the bed and breakfast and jump out to grab Sandra's luggage.

"Come on," I order her when she remains standing next to the cart.

"This is actually quite charming." She sounds surprised.

Was she always such a snob? No, I'm sure she wasn't. When we first got together in college, she wore second-hand clothes. Second-hand clothes she'd redesigned and refashioned to be similar to whatever was in style, but there were still second-hand.

"Let's get you checked in. Unless I can convince you to leave town immediately."

She purses her lips. I guess not.

I follow her into the inn and breathe a sigh of relief when I find Soleil sitting behind the front desk.

"Rowan," she greets me before pursing her lips at Sandra. "And guest."

"Hi, Soleil. Good to see you." Soleil is the same age as Aspen. Thus, two years older than me. She's a potter and conducts pottery workshops during the tourist season. During the off-season, she's similar to Ash – doing odd jobs here and there to keep herself busy.

"Soleil. What kind of name is Soleil?"

I glare at Sandra. "She's checking in."

"Alone?" Soleil asks and I imagine the news of my ex-wife checking into the inn will spread across Winter Falls before I'm back in my golf cart.

"Yes, alone."

"For how long?"

I cock an eyebrow at Sandra.

"For however long it takes," she says.

"Apparently, she's checking in until hell freezes over."

Soleil giggles but when Sandra shoots daggers out of her eyes at her, she covers her mouth and pretends to cough.

"I'll need a credit card to guarantee payment."

I stick my hands in my pockets while Sandra taps her foot. I whistle and watch the seconds tick by on the clock. I'll be damned if she's staying here on my dime. I don't want her here, and I'm certainly not paying for the displeasure of having her near.

"Oh, for heaven's sake," she grumbles before fishing her pocketbook out of her purse. She removes a credit card and slaps it on the desk. "Here."

Soleil can't hide her smile now and she's obviously not bothering to try. "Here you go," she says as she glides the room pass across the desk. "Your room is on the second floor. Do you need help with your luggage?"

"Obviously. I'm not carrying it up myself."

Does Sandra have any idea what an entitled jackass she sounds like? Guessing by her nose stuck up in the air, I'd say she does not.

"I'm out of here."

"But we need to talk," Sandra whines.

"No," I tell her. "You need to come to grips with the fact that I don't want you back."

Soleil bursts into laughter. When Sandra glares at her, she rushes off waving her hands and muttering about coming back for the luggage in a minute.

"The people in this town are strange."

I lock my jaw before I answer her. Answering her will only lead to an argument. I don't have time for an argument. I need to get back to Ashlyn before she decides to burn my house down. I wish I were exaggerating. And I wish I could fault her. I can't. Sandra isn't the only jackass in town.

I wave and walk away before she can speak again and draw me into conversation. I push the limits of the golf cart on the way home. As soon as I'm in the driveway, I leap out and run to my front door. I rush inside.

"Ash, where are you?"

When she doesn't answer, I go searching for her. The kitchen and living room are empty, as is her bedroom. I peek inside the closet but she's not there either. The bathroom door is hanging open, but no one's inside. I finally check the guest room and discover the window wide open and the screen off. Weird but whatever.

I could search the town for Ash, but if she doesn't want to be found, she won't be. I guess our talk will have to wait. Maybe the reprieve will give me a chance to figure out what I'm going to say. And maybe I'm telling myself whatever's necessary to give myself an excuse to stall before we have our conversation.

I check my watch. Two o'clock. In the meantime, I'll get back to the bakery and make sure Bryan hasn't given all the food away. Unfortunately, I'm not joking. He once decided to give a free cupcake to anyone who could tell him a dirty joke. As if a dirty joke is a challenge for anyone in this town.

I return to the bakery, but after an hour, Bryan kicks me out for being grumpy. Being grumpy is not a communicable disease no matter what he claims.

I hurry home, but Ash hasn't returned yet. Where the hell is she? I asked everyone who came into the bakery, but no one seems to know where she is. Should I be out canvassing the town for her? Is she lying in a ditch somewhere? It's not normal for no one to know where the youngest West sister is.

I'm done waiting for her. I find my phone and scroll down until I reach her name. And I scroll and scroll. Shit. Ash's number isn't in my phone. Why don't I have her number?

Ah, yes. Because I was determined to not get caught in her web. I guess that ship has sailed. I tap on Lyric's name instead.

"Do you have Ash's phone number?" I ask before he can say hello.

He chuckles. "About damn time. I'll message it to you," he says and hangs up.

About time? I ignore whatever insinuation he's trying to make. Now is not the moment to revisit my hang-ups about having a relationship with anyone, let alone Ash. Hell, my hang-up drove into town today and is currently staying at the inn.

My phone beeps with a message. Ash's number. I immediately call but no one answers. I hang up and try again. After five attempts, I give up and fling my phone onto the sofa before stalking to the window. I search the street, but there's no sign of Ash returning.

Where is she? She shouldn't be gallivanting around with a broken ankle. I don't care if she has a walking cast or not. A broken ankle is a broken ankle.

I pace the living room several times before snatching my phone to try and call her again. The call connects as my door flies open.

"Hello," Ash slurs.

I hang up before stalking to her. "I've been calling and calling. Can you not pick up the phone and let me know you're okay?"

She leans back to look up at me and nearly falls over. I rush to grab her arm to keep her steady. "You have my phone number?"

"What are you talking about? Of course, I have your phone number." I didn't until a little while ago, but I certainly do now.

She shrugs and steps away from me. "My phone's in the bedroom. I forgot to grab it when we left."

I growl. "You can't go caravanning around without a phone!"

"Caravanning around? Am I gypsy now? Do I need to worry about passing through hostile territory?"

I grit my teeth before I lash out at her again. "It's an expression."

She snorts. "An old one."

"Can you be serious for one minute?"

"Why?" She huffs. "To give you a chance to tell me about your perfect little wife? No thanks."

My perfect little wife? If she only knew.

She picks up a sofa cushion and peers underneath it. "Where is she anyway?"

"Where's who?"

"Mrs. Perky Breasts. Who else?"

"She's certainly not under the sofa."

She drops the sofa cushion as if she didn't realize what she was doing.

"She's not here," I clarify.

Her nose scrunches up and she appears confused. It's adorable. "Where is she? Did she go shopping on Main Street?"

I can't imagine any store on Main Street would meet Sandra's standards. Not because there's anything wrong with the local shops, but because Sandra is a snob with a capital S. "She's staying at the inn."

"Why?" Her eyes widen and she smacks her forehead. The action causes her to stumble onto the sofa. "She doesn't need to stay at the inn. I'll go home and she can stay here. You can share a bed with her. It's not like you haven't shared a bed with her before."

"I am not sharing a bed with her. And you're not going anywhere."

"Why not?" She hiccups before lifting her boot. "I can get around just fine now."

Because I want her to stay. Because I'm a selfish asshole who knows I can't keep her, but I don't want her to leave anyway.

When I don't respond, Ash continues, "It'll be easier for you to recon- recol- reconcile without me being a third wheel."

"I don't want her back," I grit out.

She raises an eyebrow. "Really? You checked her into the inn this afternoon because you don't want her?"

I grunt. Damnit. I knew the whole town would know about me checking my ex into the inn before I had a chance to explain to Ash.

"She won't leave. I can't kick her out of town."

She leans back on the sofa and her eyes close. "Sure, you can."

I open my mouth to respond, but she snores, and I realize she's out cold. How much did she have to drink?

My phone beeps with a message. *We brought Ashlyn back to your house. You owe us.*

I shove the phone back in my pocket – there's no responding to Aspen's crazy – before picking Ash up and carrying her to bed.

I enjoy the feel of her in my arms where I wish she belonged, but it won't last forever. Not when I finally tell her why we can't be together.

Chapter 23

Ringside seat – to have a front row view of someone acting the fool

I GROAN AS I come awake. I try opening my eyes, but they're apparently glued shut. I lift my eyebrows to force them open and pain shoots across my forehead. Ouch. Why does my mouth feel like I decided to eat a bag of cotton balls last night? Unfortunately, I know exactly how that feels. I really need to learn to stop saying yes anytime someone dares me to do something.

"There's water and aspirin on the bedside table for you," Rowan says, and I practically jolt at the sound of his gruff voice. Dang. I thought I was alone with my humiliation.

I use my fingers to force my eyes open before glancing in his direction to discover him sitting in one of the armchairs near the window alcove.

"What are you doing sitting over there? You scared me half to death." My nose wrinkles when I notice a crumpled up blanket next to him. "Did you sleep on one of the chairs?"

He shrugs.

I roll my eyes. "You could have slept on the sofa. Or, you know, at the inn with the lovely Sandra." My stomach nearly revolts at the idea of the word lovely and Sandra in the same sentence.

"I wanted to make sure you were okay."

I snort. "Dude, I'm not your little sister. You can stop with the making sure I'm okay thing."

He frowns. "I don't see you as a sister. I think I made that perfectly obvious the other night."

Oh boy, did he. My body heats up and my nipples tighten as I remember how he showed me. But then he snuck out of bed without so much as a kiss to tell me he was going to work, and his ex-wife showed up to demand him back.

I infuse cheer into my voice I'm not feeling. "True story."

He rubs a hand over his neck. "We need to talk."

I turn away. "Nope. If you're going to tell me I'm a mistake again, I'm not interested. Keep it to yourself."

"I never said you were a mistake."

"Me, the kiss, what difference does it make? It's all the same."

He kneels next to the bed. "There's a big difference."

I'm going to regret this, but I say the word anyway. "Explain."

He grasps my hand, but I wrench out of his hold. I can't handle him touching me. I'll forgive him for just about any transgression if he's touching me. When it comes to Rowan Aries Hansley, I'm easy.

He grunts but doesn't speak. "Well?" I prod. No sense waiting to have my heart broken.

"First, I should apologize."

I narrow my eyes at him. "If you apologize for taking advantage of me, I will throat punch you." I wave my fist in the air. "Don't tempt me."

He drops his chin to his chest. "Um…"

I smack his shoulder. "Don't underestimate me. You may have a freakishly strong neck, but it'll still hurt when I punch you."

I'm full of shit. My fist will have absolutely zero impact on his muscular neck. And what's up with that anyway? Who has a muscular neck? Are there exercises to train neck muscles? I get my exercise the old-fashioned way – by stumbling home when I'm too drunk to drive. Although, it's kind of a moot point since there aren't many cars in Winter Falls anyway.

He lifts his hands up in surrender. "My freakishly strong neck?"

I indicate his neck with a wave of my hand. "Have you seen yourself in the mirror? It's not normal to have muscles in your neck."

He smirks. "Maybe it only appears muscular to you because your chicken neck is weak and skinny. I'm not sure how it manages to hold up your big head."

I stick my tongue out at him. My head is not big. And a skinny neck isn't bad. I think.

My phone beeps and I check the time on it. "I should probably get up and do some work."

"Yeah, I need to get back to the bakery. Before I do, though." He clears his throat.

Here we go. Time for 'The Talk'. Yippee. I can't wait. I cross my arms over my chest and lean back against my pillow.

"I enjoyed our night together—"

"Night together?" I snort. "I think you mean sex. We had sex. Which is probably freaking you out because you think I'm your little sister and now you're having some type of crisis about being in an incestuous relationship."

"Can I talk?"

"I don't know. Can you?"

"You are such a shit stirrer."

I smile. "Thank you."

"It wasn't a compliment."

I point to his face. "Your smile says otherwise."

He wasn't actually smiling, but he is now. He cocks an eyebrow. "Will you let me talk or are you going to continue to interrupt me?"

I shrug. "I don't know. Are you going to say I'm a mistake again? Because we know how that conversation will end." I raise my fists and shadow box.

"Damnit, Ash. There's a difference between me saying us being together is a mistake and saying you're a mistake."

I wrap my arms around my waist and wait for him to explain. I hope I have enough duct tape in my arsenal to tape my heart back together when he's finished because I just know whatever he's planning to say is going to shred me.

He reaches for me, but I scoot away from him. His hand drops to the blanket.

"As I was saying, I enjoyed our night together – the sex." He waggles his eyebrows, but I give him nothing. "It was phenomenal. The best I've ever had."

I clutch my shirt to stop myself from reaching out to him at those words. I know there's a but coming and it's going to hurt.

"But we can't be together."

My heart stalls and I forget to breathe. Expecting the words didn't dim the pain whatsoever.

"Because you consider me your little sister," I manage to force the words out of my mouth.

"No. Hell no. I don't take care of you because I see you as my sister. I take care of you because I can't help myself. I need to make sure you're happy and healthy and safe."

Now, I'm confused. Those words make it sound as if he cares for me.

"But we can't be together?" Color me confused.

He doesn't hesitate. "No."

My breath hitches and he reaches for me again. I scramble to the other side of the bed. He may be freakishly tall, but this bed is obnoxiously large. Unless he crawls into it with me, which he won't, I can keep my distance from him.

"It's not you."

I growl.

"No," he's quick to recover, "I'm not going to say it's not you, it's me. I can't have a relationship with anyone."

A lightbulb goes off above me and I realize I'm the biggest idiot in the world. I nearly smack myself upside the head.

"Because you're still in love with Sandra." Duh.

He recoils. "What makes you think that?"

"Let me count the ways. One, you haven't been with anyone since you returned to town after your divorce." And yes, I would know. This is Winter Falls after all, and I do have stalkerish tendencies.

"Two, you didn't kick Sandra out of town." No, he checked her into the inn my sister owns. Did he not realize I'd find out about it before Sandra's luggage was in her room?

"And, three." I lower my voice and imitate him. "You can't have a relationship with anyone."

A muscle in his jaw ticks. "I'm not in love with Sandra."

I cross my arms over my chest. "Prove it."

"Okay. How?"

Crap. I didn't think he'd agree. Now what?

"Kick her out of town."

"I'm not the Chief of Police. I can't simply get rid of someone because I don't want her here."

Damn. He's right. I'm not backing down, though. The words 'back down' are not in my vocabulary.

I throw the covers off of me to discover I'm still dressed. What did I do? Pass out in my clothes? Apparently so.

"You'll figure out a way," I tell him. "In the meantime, I need to get to work."

I'm lying. I finished all my projects early, but I can always use the time to update my website and do some marketing to find new clients.

"Ash," he pleads.

I hold up a hand to stop whatever words are going to come out of his mouth.

"Nope. I don't want to hear it. Actions speak louder than words."

I march into the bathroom. I nearly slam the door behind me, but I don't want Rowan to know how much his unwillingness to move forward with a relationship with me is hurting me even though it's killing me. I shut the door and lean against it.

Only when I hear his footsteps retreating from the room do I slide to the floor and bury my face in my hands. I inhale through my nose and exhale out through my mouth the way I learned in that stupid meditation class I was forced to attend in college because of a fight I did not cause. It doesn't help.

Tears leak out of my eyes and my heart rate skyrockets until I'm the picture of a blubbering fool on the floor of the bathroom. I knew this would happen. I knew living with Rowan – albeit temporarily – would destroy me. And I did it anyway. I'm such a fool.

No more, Ashlyn. No more. Put on your big girl panties. It's time to commence Project Forget Rowan Ever Existed. I'll get right on that. Just as soon as I can stop my eyes from leaking and my heart from breaking into a million pieces.

Chapter 24

Beat someone to the punch – when your mom anticipates your response before you realize what your response is going to be

I PAUSE WITH MY hand on the doorknob. *Come on, Ash.* You can do this. You can be in the same room as Rowan and not kill him. Snort. I wish I wanted to kill him. But no. No matter how much he hurt my heart, I still want to jump him like he's a tall glass of water I found after I trekked over the desert for days without anything to drink. Why I would trek over the desert is beyond me, but my comment stands.

I straighten my back and throw the door open. I march down the hallway through the living room on my way out the door. Trust me, I did consider jumping out of the window, but once was enough. This boot doesn't exactly invite aerobatic displays.

"Hold up!" Rowan shouts before rushing to me.

I keep my back to him. If I don't see his face, I won't crave him. I lie. I can feel his energy in the room, and I want to suck it up and drown in it.

"What?" I manage to ask without sounding all breathy.

"I'll drive you."

I whirl around. "You don't know where I'm going."

He smirks. "Yeah, I do. It's Sunday. You're going to Sunday family dinner."

Apparently, I'm not only a mistake, I'm predictable. My self-confidence is going to need an electric shock to restart it once I move back home.

"Whatever," I mumble.

I'm not going to argue with him. Arguing with him means I have to spend more time in his presence and I'm not afraid to admit being in his presence makes me want to forgive him despite the whole 'have sex with her but afterwards tell her you don't want a relationship' thing.

He places his hand on my lower back to escort me out of the house and I jolt forward before I rush away. I probably resemble a maniac the way I'm bustling in my boot toward the golf cart, but I don't care. Much.

"How is your work going?" Rowan asks as we drive the few blocks to my parents' house.

I contemplate not answering for a count of thirty but finally settle on, "Fine."

He clenches his jaw. I guess he's not a total idiot. He knows fine is the worst possible answer a woman can give a man. Lucky for him, he decides to forego any further conversation attempts for the remainder of the three-minute drive.

The second he rolls to a stop in front of my parents' house, I hop out of the cart and wave. "Thanks for the ride, Jeeves." I frown when he switches off the engine and exits the vehicle. "What are you doing? I'm perfectly safe here."

I hear the door open behind me. "Rowan!" Aspen greets. "You made it."

I'm going to kill my sister. I'm sure there's some kind of defense to murder when the victim is your sister and she's being a pain in your ass. Any juror who has siblings will understand.

"Vengeance is in my heart, death in my hand. Blood and revenge are hammering in my head," I grumble as I pass her into the house.

"Drama nerd!" She yells after me.

"Dead woman walking!" I yell back.

"Ashlyn Dream." Mom smiles as I enter the dining room and pulls me into her arms for a hug. I'm not a baby, but I admit I lean into her for a moment. What can I say? She gives the best hugs, and I could certainly use one now. "I'm glad you could make it."

Make it? I'm here every Sunday. Before I can respond, she releases me and opens her arms to hug Rowan.

"Thank you for coming."

"Thank you for inviting me, Mrs. West."

She giggles. "Don't be silly. Call me Ruby." She winks at him, and my eyes roll so far back in my head, I think they're going to get stuck there.

"It's been a long time since I've eaten a homecooked meal I didn't make myself. And it's been entirely too long since I've eaten your world famous fried chicken and coleslaw." What a suck-up.

Mom's chest puffs out. "Thank you, my dear. How are your parents doing in Florida?"

He chuckles. "As well as two hippies in Florida can do, I guess. Dad's trying to convince everyone to install solar panels and Mom's serving hash brownies at book club."

Lyric arrives and slaps Rowan on the back. "Hey, man. Good to see you." He lowers his voice and adds, "It's about damn time."

About damn time for what? I study the two of them, but they don't give anything away with their manly posturing.

"Are they going to grunt at each other while scratching their armpits?" Lilac asks as she joins me.

"Why do men do the whole pounding of their chest thing?" Juniper asks.

"Well," Lilac begins, but Juniper shoves her hand in Lilac's face.

"I was joking."

"Whatever," Lilac huffs before marching to the kitchen to help with the food.

Dad enters the room and smiles when he sees me. He ruffles my hair. "Good to see you, baby girl. How are you doing? How's the ankle?"

"It's fine. I'm ready to get this walking cast off yesterday."

"You can't rush a recovery," Dad lectures.

"Which is what I've been trying to tell her," Rowan adds.

I scan the area as if I can't see Rowan standing right in front of me, "Did anyone hear someone speak? I think we have a ghost."

Dad chuckles before leaning close to kiss my cheek. "Don't give him too hard of a time."

If he only knew. But he won't. My dad may give the impression of a gentle bumbling bear, but you don't mess with his girls.

Mom claps her hands. "Everyone be seated, please." She indicates a chair on the far end. "Rowan, you sit there next to Ashlyn."

I glare at Mom. She rolls her eyes. "You had sex with the man. Surely, you can sit next to him for a meal."

My cheeks warm until I'm sure they're the color of a fire hydrant. "Mom."

"What? Are you ashamed? Do I need to have the talk about not being ashamed to have sex with you again?"

"No," I grit out.

"In that case, sit down." She motions to the chair next to where Rowan is already sitting.

I plop down next to the man who's not bothering to hide his amusement. "How can you think this is funny?"

"Because she's not my mom and everyone's staring at you and not me," he explains.

Stupid common sense explanation. "Whatever."

Yep. I've turned into a petulant child. Way to show Rowan you're a woman and he's missing out by not wanting to have a relationship with you.

"Did you watch the Broncos game last week?" Lyric asks, and I want to fall at his feet to thank him for changing the topic of conversation.

"It was a good game, but the real test will be the game next Sunday."

Lyric nods. "I can't wait for the game. I gave both Peace and Freedom duty, so I won't be disturbed. They weren't amused."

"You should come over to our place to watch the game. In fact, you should all come. We'll have a little football party."

Our place? Did he forget we're not in a relationship? I won't be reminding him of our non-relationship status in front of the family, though. Better to stick to my living with him as a temporary arrangement.

"I might be out of my cast by then. I'm hoping the doctor can move my next appointment up." Rowan doesn't respond, so I nudge him. "If I can finally get this thing off, I'll be back home with Juniper."

"There's no hurry to rush home on my account," Juniper's quick to say.

I glare at her. She already won the when will Ashlyn and Rowan get sweaty between the sheets bet. Why doesn't she want me to come home? I groan. Don't tell me there's another bet. A bet she's sure to lose.

Mom and Lilac enter the room and set platters of fried chicken, coleslaw, and green salad on the table. "Dig in, everyone."

While everyone else dives on the food like they haven't eaten in years, I narrow my eyes on Juniper and mouth *I will get you back.*

She wiggles her fingers at me, completely unconcerned. She should be concerned. Two can play at this game. And I happen to know there's a game afoot with Juniper. A game she thinks I don't know about, but I do.

"This chicken is delicious, Ruby," Rowan mutters between bites.

"Thank you, Rowan. You'll have to join us for Sunday dinner again. Family's always welcome."

Lyric chuckles and I kick his shin. "Ow. What did I do?"

"You exist. Does there need to be a reason?"

He throws an arm around Aspen. "You're right, Sunshine. Sisters are worse than brothers."

"I don't know. Brothers can be a pain in the ass, too," Rowan says.

"How is Cedar?" Dad asks.

Rowan shrugs. "It's Cedar."

Everyone around the table nods as if they understand because we do. Cedar is Rowan's little brother. He was in Lilac's grade in school, although he barely attended any classes. Cedar was always difficult to pin down.

Last I heard, he's traveling around the country in an RV. I have no idea how he pays his bills, but I wouldn't be surprised if Rowan subsidizes him. Rowan was always helping Cedar out of scrapes when we were growing up.

Everyone returns to their food and conversation is limited to small talk about the weather and how much cheese the goats of Lyric's brother, Phoenix, can produce. The goat cheese is in high demand especially now with Aspen selling it in the bookstore. It sounds weird to sell cheese in a bookstore, but Aspen's tourist corner sells all the local produce and it's doing remarkably well.

When we finish the meal, I can't get out of here quick enough. Navigating conversation with Rowan sitting next to me is equivalent to skipping through a field filled with landmines. Especially since I don't want anyone to know about our last conversation. The one when he broke my heart.

I'll tell my sisters eventually, but not until I can have the talk without breaking down into big, blubbering sobs. No one likes an ugly crier.

I say the one thing I know will get Rowan to leave. "I should probably go rest my ankle."

As expected, he jumps out of his chair and motions to the door. Before I can make it there, Mom pulls me in close for a hug. "He has his reasons for hurting you, darling girl. Find out what they are and eliminate them."

How does she know he broke my heart? Is she psychic? I should know better than to try to keep secrets from her. She always finds out everything. Dad's parents are the Soviet defectors, but I swear Mom is the spy genius. Her talents are wasted on being a high school principal. Those poor students.

"Whatever," I mumble since I have no plan to tell her how Rowan's in love with his ex-wife.

Unfortunately, I can hardly 'eliminate' Sandra, although I admit the idea has appeal. But what if I could help Rowan get over her?

Dang it. Now I'm considering how to help Rowan. Stupid girl. You aren't a heroine in one of Juniper's romcom movies. You can't 'cure' the hero.

I wish I could say I'll heed my own advice, but I probably won't.

Chapter 25

Drop the gloves – engage in a fight with someone no matter how much you don't actually want to talk to said someone

ROWAN

Bryan enters the bakery kitchen and stops dead in his tracks when he sees me. His gaze roams over me as he appraises me. "Someone got up on the wrong side of the bed this morning."

I grunt.

He wags a finger at me. "Nuh-uh. I'm not your girl, Ashlyn. I can't interpret your grunts."

She's not my girl. Damn. I wish she were, but she can't be. I can't make a woman happy, and Ash deserves to be happy and have all her wishes come true.

"I'm fine," I tell him instead of explaining all the thoughts rattling around my brain.

He huffs. "You are not fine. You're doing it again."

"What? Baking?" I pretend I don't know what he's talking about.

He ignores my response. I can't blame him. It was pretty asinine. "You've got the whole 'I don't deserve a woman' appearance on your face. Me big man. Me caveman." He pounds his chest with his fists, but I'm not finding any humor in his drama act this morning.

"It's true," I admit to the buttercream frosting I'm using to decorate a tray of cupcakes.

"P-lease. You can't judge your worthiness based on a marriage to Sandra the Queen Bee of the bitch squad."

"I'm not."

He crosses his arms over his chest and taps his toe. "You're not?" *Tap. Tap. Tap.* Goes his toe. "Your ex-wife is literally the only woman you've been in a long-term relationship with. If she's not the cause of your ludicrous ideas about your self worth, what else could it possibly be?"

I glance up from the cupcakes to frown at him. "Sometimes I wonder why I befriended you in college."

He pops his hip out and flicks a hand next to his ear. "Because I'm awesome. Duh."

"Or I'm a sucker for a person being bullied."

His lips purse. "I hate bullies."

The only people who don't hate bullies are bullies.

"No one deserves to be mistreated because of their sexual orientation. You didn't choose to be gay."

"No." He flips his hair. "But I did choose to be fabulous."

The corners of my lips tip up in a smile.

"Since we've now established I'm fabulous, can we move on to what you're going to do to win Ashlyn back?"

I'm not winning Ash back. I need to set her free to find her happiness.

The kitchen timer goes off to indicate my bread is ready to be taken out of the oven, which means it's opening time. "Time to get to work, Mr. Fabulous."

He sighs. "This conversation is not over."

Yeah, it is.

He flounces off while I remove the bread from the oven. I arrange the various buns and loaves on a tray before entering the bakery with them.

The line is out the door, so once I'm finished replenishing the display, I join Bryan to help with the customers.

"Next!" I shout and look up from the cash register to find my worst nightmare has arrived. "What can I get you, Sandra?"

"You know I don't eat carbs."

"We have several low carb options." I hand her a menu. "Feel free to peruse the various options while I help the next customer."

She slaps the menu on the counter. "No! You will listen to me and hear me out."

I place my hands on my hips. "I'm kind of busy here. I don't come to your place of work and disturb you, do I? Oh wait. That's right. You don't work."

"Burn!" Soleil squeals from behind my ex.

I crane my neck to peek behind her and notice she's not alone. Ellery is with her. Great. This confrontation is going to get back to Ash before it can begin. I know I told Ash we can't be together, but it doesn't mean I'm a total asshole who doesn't realize my ex being around is hurting her.

"Why are you still in town?"

She tilts her chin in the air. "I told you. I'm not leaving until I get what I came for."

"What did she come for?" Feather asks.

"Apparently, she wants Rowan back," Soleil answers. "But he told her hell would freeze over first."

I'm certain Feather already knows about the conversation Sandra and I had when she checked into the inn but, guessing by the twinkle in Soleil's eyes, she's enjoying rubbing it in Sandra's nose.

"Mind your own business. This is private," Sandra tells the crowd.

"Hey! We're not the ones who decided to conduct a private conversation in front of the whole town," Petal points out.

"Can you take a break?" Sandra asks me.

I motion to the line behind her. "Does it look like I have time for a break?"

"We need to talk, but you've been avoiding me."

Damn straight I have. I want nothing to do with the woman standing in front of me. I can't believe I stayed married to her for as long as I did. I blame my lapse of judgment on being young and getting drafted in the NFL. You hear your name picked and all common sense flies out the window for at least two years.

"I have nothing to say to you."

She sticks out her bottom lip in a pout. Does she think any of her old tricks are going to work on me? Not a chance in hell when my dream woman is currently living in my house.

"You begged me not to divorce you," she says.

Awesome. I wanted everyone in town to know how big of an idiot I was. Thanks.

"Because I believe marriage is forever."

My marriage was over long before the defensive end tackled me and destroyed my knee and career, but I still thought I should work on my relationship with Sandra. I wasn't ready to admit defeat. I never am. And I certainly wasn't prepared to deal with a divorce while I was convalescing and learning to walk again.

"Good. We can start where we left off."

"I believe where we left off was you leaving." I indicate the door. "Don't let it hit you on the way out."

Bryan cheers. "Go, Rowan." He pretends to have pompoms in his hands as he cheers. "Get rid of the trash. There you go." Feather, Petal, and Sage cheer him on from the sidelines.

Sandra glares at him. "Wonderful. Bryan's here. I should have known he followed you here. He always was such a devoted little puppy."

"At least, I know how to be loyal," Bryan fires back at her.

"I never cheated," she insists.

He sniffs. "Depends on how you define cheat."

What's he getting at? We had a metric ton of issues in our relationship, but infidelity wasn't one of them.

She snorts. "As if gay men know what cheating means."

The vibe of the crowd changes from amused to angry in a split second. Winter Falls tolerates many things, but they don't tolerate judgment. As Mrs. West would say, this is a judgment-free town.

"Who votes to run her out of town?" Sage asks and every single person in the bakery – and the place is packed – raises their hand.

"Where does the chief keep the pitchforks?" Feather asks Sage. As the police dispatcher, Sage would know.

"I don't need no damn pitchfork." Forest elbows his way to the front of the crowd. "Your behavior will not be tolerated in Winter Falls. Do you understand?" he asks her.

She assesses him and her nose wrinkles. Admittedly, Forest doesn't project the best picture with his overgrown hair and unkempt beard. At least he's wearing pants today. "Who do you think you are?"

"I'm the mayor of Winter Falls," he announces as if being the mayor is a big deal.

It's not. We don't hold elections for mayor in this town. We put the names of the business owners into a hat and pick one. The person picked has to serve for one year, but no one is obliged to serve two consecutive terms.

"I didn't mean to upset anyone. Bryan and I go way back."

Bryan snorts behind me. "Frenemies from the start."

If I had only listened to him when he told me Sandra was trouble. Once again, I'm blaming the being young thing. Young men are idiots. The proof is standing right in front of me.

Forest crosses his arms over his chest and glares down at her. "I think your welcome here has worn out."

"The mayor doesn't have authority to run anyone out of town," Sandra insists.

"Maybe not. But I do," Lyric says as he enters.

I lift my chin at him in greeting.

"The owner of every establishment in Winter Falls has the right to refuse a customer service. I think the owner has made it clear he's refusing you service," he explains as he grasps her arm and starts hauling her away.

She wrenches out of his hold. "Do not touch me. I know when I'm not wanted."

"You could have fooled me," Bryan mumbles behind me. I motion for him to be quiet. She's on her way out the door. I don't want to give her an excuse to stay.

Sandra lifts her nose in the air and marches away. Unlike with Lyric, the crowd doesn't part for her. She has to push and shove her way through the mass. When she finally reaches the door, cheers erupt.

She stomps down the sidewalk, but I fear this isn't the last I've seen of her. Sandra never could take no for an answer. As I watch, Ellery moves to follow her.

"Ellery," I shout to gain her attention.

"Don't worry. I won't tell, Ash." She sweeps her arm out to indicate the people who are already on their phones. "But they will."

The stupid town Facebook page. Damnit! News already spread like wildfire before the town discovered social media. I never would have thought the gossiping in this town could get worse when I left for college, but it did.

Chapter 26

End around – an evasive tactic sometimes used to get a person's mind off of their obsession

"Let's go."

I glance up from my computer to find Aspen standing at the entrance to the walk-in closet.

"Go? Where are we going? What are we doing?"

I know we don't have any plans for today. It's the middle of the week. Aspen should be at her bookstore.

"Get a move on. I haven't got all day," she says instead of answering my questions.

I return my attention to my computer where I've been Googling how to help a man move on after divorce. Yep. I'm a total loser who's not only going to forgive Rowan for being a complete and utter idiot but also figure out how to convince him to get over Sandra and have a relationship with me.

Aspen marches over and slams my computer shut. "Now. Get up. And put some clothes on." She hauls me to my feet.

I wrench my arm free of her hold. "I'm dressed," I protest.

"A pajama top and leggings is not dressed." Her nose wrinkles as she studies me. "And it wouldn't hurt to brush your hair and wash your face either."

"No." I cross my arms over my chest. "Tell me what we're doing first."

She smirks. "We're going to visit Mercury."

"Old Man Mercury?"

"Is there another Mercury in this town?"

A visit to Mercury can only mean one thing – time to work on the mystery.

"Why didn't you say so to start with?" I push past her. "I'll shower quick as can be and get dressed." Because I lied. I am in my pajamas.

I rush through the world's fastest shower. "What's the plan?" I ask as I throw on a pair of jeans.

"I figure if anyone knows anything about a newspaper from 1955 when the Black Hat Bandit and Patricia were supposed to meet up then he will."

I put on my boot and stand. "Let's go."

Aspen gestures toward my upper half. "Maybe you want to wear a shirt over your bra. Just a suggestion."

Oops. Guess I'm a bit overexcited about finding the loot. Just imagine all the things I could do with half a million dollars. Buy a house. Build a sound booth. The possibilities are endless!

Since Mercury's house is on the outer limits of town, we drive a golf cart there. Like most residents of Winter Falls, I'm convinced the house is haunted. I tried holding a séance in his yard once to summon the ghosts – or demons, I'm not fussy –

but apparently, there's more to holding a séance than wrapping your mom's old skirt around your head and throwing a sheet over a basketball.

In my defense, Mom wouldn't allow me to have a computer at home until I was in high school. It's hard to Google 'how to hold a séance' on a school computer when your mom's a teacher there.

"Has Mercury been doing repairs on his place?" I ask as we park in front of his house, and I notice the stairs leading up to the porch appear new and the railing's been recently painted.

Aspen blushes. "Not Mercury."

"You built stairs?"

"Don't be silly. Lyric did the stairs. I painted."

"But why?"

"I don't know. I have the feeling Mercury's story is tragic."

My jaw drops. "Oh, my word! You want to convince him to write his memoir, don't you?"

She shrugs. "Maybe."

"You won't ask him about it today, you hear me?" I order her. " Today, we're on a treasure hunt."

"I know," she practically squeals.

My big sis is always up for an adventure. It's one of the reasons why she left town after she graduated college. But since she's now engaged to her childhood sweetheart, she's back to stay. Yeah!

The door creaks open and Mercury steps out onto the porch. "Are you going to sit out here gossiping all day or are you coming in?"

His crotchety old man ways don't bother Aspen one bit. She smiles up at him. "Good morning, Mercury."

He grunts before going back inside.

"Let's go," she says but I'm already out of the cart and on the stairs.

We follow Mercury into the house and settle at the kitchen table. He doesn't bother with small talk. "What have you got for me today?"

Aspen pulls the letter out of her bag and slides it across the table to show him. "We found this letter in the safe at the brewery. It's addressed to Patricia from Robert."

Mercury scans the letter. "You'll find the item referred to in the temporary tablecloth," he reads aloud. "And you figure 'the item referred to' is the money he stole from the bank?"

"Yeah." I rub my hands together as my excitement builds. "And I think the temporary tablecloth is a newspaper, but I don't know what newspaper it could be since the *Winter Falls Post* wasn't established until 1960 and the letter was written in February of 1955."

Mercury studies me for a long moment. "There's more to you than being a troublemaker, Ashlyn Dream."

I don't bristle at being referred to as a troublemaker. Not when he obviously means his words as a compliment. "Thank you."

"Do you have any idea what newspaper the Black Hat Bandit is referring to?" Aspen asks.

Mercury smiles and it transforms his face. He seems decades younger, although I have no idea how old he is in reality.

"I can do you one better," he says and stands. "Come on."

I jump to my feet and rush after him. He opens a door, and we descend a flight of stairs to his basement, which is filled to the rim with boxes. There's barely room to breathe down here. I notice several boxes labeled Adhara. What's Adhara?

"Here it is," Mercury announces. He taps a box labeled Clifton.

"Clifton?" I ask. "As in the previous owner of the mansion?"

"Someone read my book," he mumbles. "Bring the box upstairs," he orders before shuffling away.

I reach for the box, but Aspen elbows me out of the way. "Rowan would kill me if I let you carry a box."

"And Lyric won't kill me?"

"I don't have a broken ankle."

Oh, yeah. I forgot about my stupid ankle for a minute there despite the heavy boot clomping around as I walk. I trail after Aspen as she carries the box up the stairs and sets it on the kitchen table.

"What's in here?" I ask.

"Hold your horses, young lady," Mercury snaps.

"My horses are being held," I snap back.

He chuckles as he opens the box. I peer inside. It's filled with newspapers. I lean closer. *The Winter Creek Bulletin.*

"Winter Creek?" asks Aspen.

"The name of the settlement before it became Winter Falls," I tell her.

"The *Winter Creek Bulletin* was a weekly newsletter," Mercury explains as he rifles through the pile. "Clifton kept copies of each bulletin. When he passed away, I boxed them up and kept them."

He pulls several newspapers out. "Here are all the issues for February and March of 1955."

"Let's divide and conquer," I say and grab the top newspaper.

"What are we searching for?" Aspen asks.

"We'll know it when we find it," I mumble as I scan the document. I flip through the pages until I reach the last one. Lost and found. Yes! This is it! "Check the lost and found items on the back page."

I don't find anything interesting in the newspaper I'm reading – unless you consider losing sheep is interesting – and toss it aside for another issue. I flip to the back page and glide my finger down the list of found items. I pause when an item catches my attention. It reads like a puzzle.

"Found Item," I read aloud. "Where one might find a date at the imposing residence." I pause for dramatic purpose – I did study drama after all – before squealing, "This is it!"

"But what does it mean?" Aspen asks.

"Imposing residence obviously refers to the old mansion," I say. "But what does where one might find a date mean?"

"Hold on." Aspen fishes out her phone. "I know a website for crossword clues."

Mercury clears his throat. "I don't need no dang phone to tell you it means cornerstone."

"What's a cornerstone?"

"An important quality or feature on which a particular thing depends or is based," Aspen reads off her phone. "I'm confused. Wait. There's a second definition. A stone that forms the base of a corner of a building, joining two walls."

"But what does it have to do with dates?" I ask.

"The cornerstone is the first stone set in the construction of a masonry foundation," Mercury explains. "The stone often indicates the construction dates of the building."

"Do you think the Black Hat Bandit hid the money in the cornerstone? It doesn't make sense. The mansion was already built in 1955."

Aspen snaps a picture of the found ad. "I don't know, but we're going to find out."

"Thanks for your help, Mercury," I tell him as we stand to leave.

Aspen rushes around to kiss his cheek. "Thank you."

"Ellery is not going to be amused if we dig up the lawn at the inn," I say once we're in the golf cart traveling back to town.

"It's a struggle for another day. I need to drop you off and get back to the store. My lunch break is nearly over."

Lucky for me, I don't need Aspen to continue on my quest.

She shakes her finger at me. "Nuh-uh. You aren't going to the inn without me."

What she doesn't know won't hurt her.

She holds out her pinky. "Sister pinky swear."

Damnit. I can't break a sister pinky swear. I sigh before looping my pinky with hers.

"Say it," she demands.

"I sister pinky swear I won't go to the inn without you."

When she stops in front of Rowan's house, I hop out and wave as I make my way toward the door.

"By the way, Sandra stopped by the bakery and got into a fight with Rowan this morning." She beeps her horn and drives off as if she didn't just drop a bomb while I stand there with my mouth hanging open.

I snap my mouth shut before stomping toward the house. Stupid Sandra. How the hell am I going to convince Rowan to give me a chance when the woman he's hung up on won't leave town?

But is he really hung up on her? As far as I know, he hasn't gone to visit her since she's been in Winter Falls. And he claims he doesn't love her anymore. Time to find out the truth.

Chapter 27

Full-court press – pulling out all the stops for the win

OPERATION 'CONVINCE ROWAN TO GIVE ASH A CHANCE' is in full swing. And by full swing, I mean I'm sitting in the living room waiting for Rowan's return to confront him. If he won't tell me why we can't be together, I'll have to resort to other measures.

Thus far, the list of 'other measures' includes sauntering around the house naked until he can't help but ravish me and blackmailing Bryan to confess all Rowan's deepest, darkest secrets. Blackmailing as in switching off his Wi-Fi at home, so he can't watch the finale of *RuPaul's Drag Race.* Mean, I know. But when needs must.

Since I'm not quite ready to go full naked in the house all the time, I'm wearing as little clothing as possible. I've got my tightest tank top on. It's short and shows off my midriff. On the bottom, I'm wearing a pair of short shorts. I wiggle as the shorts creep up my ass. Frankly, being naked would be more comfortable at this point.

The door opens, and Rowan strides inside. Too late to change now.

I stand and approach him. His eyes flare as he takes in my outfit. My plan is working perfectly thus far.

"Are you okay?"

The flame in his eyes dies and his brow furrows. "Am I okay? Why wouldn't I be?"

"Maybe because your ex confronted you at the bakery this morning."

He blows out a puff of air. "Heard about that, did you?"

"It's Winter Falls. You're lucky I didn't show up at the bakery while she was there." And I would have. Had I known she was there. Unfortunately, I switch my phone off while I'm recording. And then Aspen showed off and pulled off a distraction. It was a fun distraction, but I'm still planning my revenge on her.

When he doesn't respond, I pull up my big girl panties and ask, "What? You said you didn't want her in town. Maybe you won't kick her out, but I will. Unless you lied and you do want her here."

I hold my breath as I wait for his answer. He doesn't make me wait long.

"Hell no." Judging by the venom in his voice, he's not lying.

I need to be certain, though. "You're sure?"

"I kicked the woman out of the bakery in front of the whole town. What more evidence do you need?"

Phew. Step one of the plan is finished. Put a checkmark next to 'confirm Rowan is not still in love with bitchy ex-wife'. Onto step two – aka 'force the stubborn man to tell me why he doesn't want a relationship'.

I point to the sofa. "Shall we sit?"

"What's going on?"

"We need to talk."

At the word 'talk', he groans. "What about?"

"Sit and I'll tell you."

He settles on the sofa. "Hit me."

I'm not one for beating around the bush, so I hit him with the most important question. "If you're not in love with the Queen Bitch, why can't you have a relationship with me?"

"I can't have a relationship with anyone."

"Explain."

He glances away. "I can't."

Guess I'll have to resort to other measures to convince him to tell me the reason. I crawl onto his lap and straddle him.

"What are you doing?"

I bat my eyelashes. "Me? Nothing. Why?"

He grunts.

I poke his chest. "Don't call me a liar."

"I didn't say anything."

"I heard your grunt."

I wiggle on his lap until I'm comfortable. His eyes fall closed, and he moans. His hands grab my hips, and his fingertips dig in. "You need to stop, my little temptress."

I've never been called a temptress before. I like it. I bite my lip. "I'll stop as soon as you tell me why you won't give us a chance."

His fingers flex on my hips. "You promise?"

I bite my lip and trail a finger down his chest. "Unless you don't want me to stop."

He snatches my finger before I can reach the snap of his jeans.

"Stop tempting me and I'll tell you."

I clear my throat and lean back. "Listening Ashlyn is ready and waiting."

He stares at me for a moment before admitting, "I can't make a woman happy."

I wait for more, but apparently, this is it. "You're joking?"

"I'm not joking. I can't be with you because I can't make you happy."

I bark out a laugh. "I think you're confused. You made me happy – twice if I recall – the other night."

"Sex isn't the problem."

"Then, what is?"

"I told you. I can't make a woman happy."

"What are you basing this stupid ass idea on? Your marriage to Mrs. Queen Bitch?"

He frowns before glancing away.

I slap his shoulder. "You are! Dude, you should know better. No one can make Queen Bitch happy. It's how she earned the title Queen of all the bitches. Hell, she was probably born with a scowl on her face."

He lifts me off his lap and stands. "I'm telling you, Ash. I can't make you happy. I refuse to enter into a relationship when I know it's doomed from the start."

"When did you become a fortune-teller? And can you give me the numbers for this weekend's lottery?"

"Don't make light of the matter. I'm being serious."

"I'm sorry, but I find it hard to be serious when you just keep repeating the same words over and over again. And the words you're repeating constitute one of the most insane things I've ever heard, and I grew up in Winter Falls."

"This discussion is over," he says and tries to walk away.

I wrap my arms around his waist to stop him. "Nope. You're not leaving here until you tell me the truth."

"I am telling you the truth," he grits out.

"Not the entire truth."

Because he has to be holding something back. People get divorced all the time. They don't stop living because their spouse becomes a money grubbing she-devil. A money grubbing she-devil with excellent bone structure and good taste in clothes, but a she-devil nonetheless.

His sigh is loud and long before he finally speaks. "Do you want children?"

"What? Did I enter a parallel universe? You won't date me, but you want to discuss having children with me?"

"It's the whole point, Ash. I can't have children."

He peels my arms from around him and starts marching away again. Not on my watch he won't.

"That's it?" I shout after him. "That's the whole reason you've been avoiding me for the past year and are afraid to enter a relationship with me? Because you can't have children? I call bullshit."

He whirls around. "It's not bullshit, Ash. I know you. You want the entire dream – a house with a white picket fence—"

"Ugh. Not white. Do you know how often you have to paint a fence when it's white?"

"Be serious for once in your life, Ashlyn!"

Uh oh. He used my full name. He's mad. Guess what? He may be mad, but I am downright pissed the eff off.

"Me be serious?" I pound my fist on my chest. "I'm not being serious? I'm trying to make light of the situation because if I don't, I'm going to rip your ears clean off your big, fat head."

"What are you talking about? Are you mad?"

"What was your first clue? The steam coming out of my ears?"

"How can you possibly be mad I can't have children?"

"You idiot!" I scream. "I'm not mad you can't have children. I'm sad for you. I'm sorry. I should have said so in the first place. Rowan, I'm sorry you can't have children. There. That's done. Moving on to scolding you for being a total nincompoop."

"Nincompoop. Does anyone under the age of sixty use that word?"

"Yes. Me. Shut it. I'm talking now."

He motions for me to carry on.

"One, it's not up to you to decide we can't be together because you can't have children. A relationship is by definition between two people. By making this decision unilaterally, you're implying I'm a dolt who can't make her own choices."

"I'm sorry, Ash. I didn't mean you can't make decisions for yourself."

I shove my palm in his face. "I'm not done."

"Of course, you're not," he mutters. I pretend not to hear him. I'm on a roll here.

"And, second, being unable to have children doesn't mean you can't have children." I wrinkle my nose. Talk about confusing sentences. "What I mean to say is there are other options. Adoption being at the top of the list. A sperm donor is another option. I'm sure there are fertility treatments as well, but I need to research the subject."

I mentally add 'research infertility in men' to my to-do list.

"You don't get it, Ash. I want you to have everything you want including children of your own."

"What if everything I want is standing in front of me being bullheaded?"

"I'm sorry," he whispers before walking away.

This time, I let him go. I need time to figure out how to convince him being sterile doesn't mean he can't be in a relationship. Idiot.

Chapter 28

Go the distance – carry through with an endeavor no matter how much the idea makes you want to smash your head against the wall again and again

ROWAN

"What are you doing here?" Ellery hisses when I enter *The Inn on Main*.

"I'm here to get my ex-wife to leave."

"About damn time. She's in her room plotting world domination."

I snort. "She's too lazy to dominate the world."

"Thank the heavens. No disrespect to you, but she's mean - rattlesnake biting you because it feels like it - mean."

"I am aware," I mutter before raising my voice to ask, "What room number?"

"Are you sure you want to go up there? I can ring her room and have her come down here."

"There isn't a chance in hell she'll have a conversation with me in public."

She considers me for a moment before giving in. "She's in room seven on the second floor."

I rush up the stairs. Not only do I not want anyone seeing me here before I can explain my visit to Ash, but I don't want to be here. I reach the room and knock on Sandra's door while calling out her name. "Sandra. We need to talk."

"Just a minute," she sings.

Judging by the excitement in her voice, she thinks she's won. She's probably in there now changing into 'something more comfortable'. Save me.

"I'm coming in."

I open the door and sure enough, she's digging through one of her multitude of suitcases. She spins around when she realizes I'm already in the room.

"Rowan," she simpers before sauntering toward me.

I hold up my hands. "Have a seat, Sandra. We need to talk."

"But there are much better things we can be doing." Her gaze flicks to the bed.

Is she delusional? Does she actually think I'm going to jump into bed with her after she left me while I was still in the hospital recovering from a career-ending knee surgery?

"You need to leave Winter Falls."

She sticks out her bottom lip in a pout. "Why? Are you moving?"

Is she deliberately being obtuse? "No, I'm staying and you're leaving."

"Long distance relationships don't work."

"True story," I hear Ellery whisper from the hallway where I know she's listening. I left the door open for her on purpose. I don't want Ash thinking I'm in here having sex with my ex.

"We are not having a long distance relationship. We're not having any relationship. It's what happens when two people divorce. Unless they have children." My heart squeezes at the word children.

She huffs. "You and your quest to have children. It's tiresome. I'm glad I lied to you about you being sterile, so you would stop pushing me to have children."

I must have heard her wrong. She didn't just tell me she lied about me being sterile. No, not even Sandra is that cruel.

"What did you say?"

"It's no big deal. When the doctor phoned with the results of our fertility exams, I lied and told you he said you had fertility issues. It was for your own good. You were at the height of your career. Having children would have distracted you."

I collapse in a chair and bury my face in my hands. She lied. I can have children. I've been torturing myself for years thinking I was less of a man because of a fucking lie.

My nostrils flare as I glare at her. "You bitch!"

She gasps. "How dare you?"

I stand and point at her. "No. How dare you? How dare you lie about something as important as having children? Let me guess. You wanted me to concentrate on my career to make sure I kept bringing in the millions for you to spend. Joke's on you. My career ended too soon anyway."

Her lips purse. "Yes, I'm aware."

"And yet, here you are, begging me to take you back. Leave, Sandra. Just leave. I am never taking you back. I will never for—" I cut myself off. There's no sense rehashing the past. I'm done with it and her. I stalk out of the room.

She yells after me, "I'll give you a child."

"I don't want *your* child."

Ellery gives me a thumbs-up. "I'll have her checked out within the hour."

I nod but don't stop to thank her. I've got somewhere I need to be. I sprint all the way from the inn to my house. When I rush inside, Ash's waiting for me.

"How did your talk with Sandra go? I assume well since all the chatter on the Facebook page is about her skedaddling out of town." She shakes her phone at me.

For once, I'm not annoyed with the ridiculous gossip page. I'm glad she knows my ex is on her way out of town.

I grasp her hand and lead her to the couch. "We need to talk."

She yanks out of my hold. "Wait. Let me get my research."

"Research? What are you researching?"

"Adoption. Male infertility. Sperm donation. The usual suspects when the man you love says he won't have a relationship with you because he can't have children."

My stomach warms at her words. Did she mean them? I shackle her wrist to stop her from going anywhere. "The man you love?"

She rolls her eyes. "This seriously can't be news to you. It's always been you. I've loved you forever. And I always will."

Screw the talk. I use my hold on her to draw her near. She crashes into me with an oomph. I don't give her a chance to catch her breath before my lips are crashing down on hers. When she gasps, I shove my tongue into her mouth. I need her flavor – happiness, sunshine, and chocolate – on my tongue. It's been entirely too long since I tasted her.

I thread my hands through her hair and tilt her head until it's at the angle I need to allow me to fall deeper into the kiss. Her hands clutch my ass, and I can't stop myself from shoving my erection into her stomach. She moans and lifts her leg to wrap it around my hips in response.

I lift her until her center is pressed against my hard length. I thrust into her, and her nails dig into my shoulders.

Shit. What am I doing? I'm dry humping the woman I love in the living room when there's a perfectly good bed in the next room. I slow the strokes of my tongue until I'm giving her little pecks on her lips.

"Does this mean we don't need to talk?" she asks between gasps for air.

Talk? Shit. Right. I need to explain some things to her. I loosen my hold on her waist until her legs fall. The sound of her boot hitting the floor startles me. Crap. I should be more careful with her.

"Sorry, dream girl, but we definitely need to talk."

"Do I need to get my research?"

"No." I guide her to the sofa and sit on the coffee table in front of her before gathering her hands in mine.

"Sandra lied."

She snorts. "I'm sure she lied about lots of things. Bitches are known for their lying."

I squeeze her hands. "She lied about my infertility."

Her nose scrunches up in confusion. It's adorable and I can't stop myself from leaning forward to kiss the tip.

"But how? Didn't you talk to the doctor yourself?"

"You have to understand. When you play professional football, you're on the road for weeks at a time. You rely on your spouse to handle all the home stuff while you're gone. When Sandra said the doctor told her I'm sterile, I didn't question it."

"Okay. I can see how that could happen. I guess. But why?"

"She doesn't want children. Instead of talking to me about it, she made the decision for me."

"Sounds familiar," she quips.

"Smart ass. I'm sorry. I was wrong. I shouldn't have made the decision about whether we could be together without talking to you."

"Your apology is accepted. I will, however, be billing you for the hours of research I did on male infertility and adoption."

"I'll pay you in red velvet pancakes."

"Not in sexual favors? I'm disappointed."

"The sexual favors are free," I tell her.

Her cheeks darken until they're a dusty pink. "What now?"

"Now we finish what we started a few minutes ago when you were grinding against me."

She rolls her eyes. "No. I mean yes. We will be doing more of the sexy times. A lot more, I hope." She waggles her eyebrows before becoming serious. "But I mean us. What happens with us? Are we a couple now?"

I could kick myself for how uncertain she sounds. I'm such an asshole.

"If you can forgive me for pushing you away for the past year."

She taps her chin as she studies me. "I'm not sure. I may need lots and lots of orgasms before I can decide."

"Oh, you'll be getting lots and lots of orgasms, don't you worry. But not until you forgive me. I don't want to have this hanging over our heads for the rest of our lives."

"The rest of our lives?"

I shrug. "Or until you get tired of my ugly mug."

"Ugly mug? You know you're the most handsome guy in Winter Falls."

"Just Winter Falls?" I tease.

"Whatever." She takes a deep breath before letting it out. "Yes, I forgive you. But if you ever think to make big decisions about us without my input again, I won't forgive you as easily."

Shit. She's going to be pissed about the surprise I'm preparing for her. Hopefully, her excitement will outweigh her anger. I shelve my concerns. The surprise isn't ready yet anyway.

"And you won't bring up what an idiot I was every time we argue," I push.

She tsks. "Rowan, Rowan, Rowan. How little you know about women. Naturally, I'm going to bring up how much of an idiot you are whenever we argue. It's my prerogative as a woman. Plus, I'm certain you'll do other idiotic things and I'll need to remind you of your past idiocy on a regular basis."

"I can live with those terms."

"Well, what are you waiting for? Ravish me, Jeeves!"

I pick her up and throw her over my shoulder before rushing to the bedroom to do exactly that. She giggles and the sound warms my heart.

Chapter 29

Homestretch – entering the final phase of your quest to capture the man of your dreams

I slap Rowan's hand when I notice him reaching with a chip into my seven-layer dip.

"Don't you dare," I growl at him.

"But it looks good." He pouts.

"And I intend for it to look absolutely perfect when our friends arrive."

He drops the chip in favor of wrapping his arms around me from behind. He bites my earlobe and I shiver. "There's no need to be nervous," he whispers into my ear.

I relax into his arms. "I know. I'm being silly. It's just…"

"Just what, dream girl?"

I take a deep breath and let it out before admitting my fears to him. "I'm afraid I'm going to wake up from this dream in which I got everything I've ever wished for. Have you ever gotten everything you ever wished for? Stupid question. You were a quarterback in the NFL. You have an honest to goodness Super Bowl ring. Of course, you have."

He twirls me around until we're facing each other and cradles my face in his hands. "Why do you think I dubbed you my dream girl?"

I roll my eyes. "Because my parents are hippies who thought giving me the middle name Dream was completely normal. Spoiler alert – it's not."

He smiles as he shakes his head. "No, Ash. Because you are my dream."

My heart stalls and my lungs forget about the whole needing oxygen to live thing. "What?" I gasp out.

He kisses the tip of my nose. "You might have been waiting forever for me to catch up to you, but I've been dreaming about having a woman as perfect as you forever."

I melt into him, and his lips touch mine in the briefest of kisses. When he pulls away, I mewl in protest and reach for him, but the door crashes open.

"Fabulous has arrived!" Bryan announces as he enters. He glances over at me and Rowan cuddled up in the kitchen and squeals. "I hope this means we've seen the last of Queen Bitch."

"I prefer money grubbing she-devil."

"I knew I liked you Ashlyn Dream West."

I merely shake my head at him as I watch a dog saunter in behind him followed by Juniper.

"Why did you bring Bark Twain with you?"

"He's been sick and throwing up this morning."

"So, you brought him with you?" I screech. "No way. He can stay on the back porch, but I'm not cleaning up dog puke."

"You never clean up dog puke," she mutters as she leads the dog outside.

"Because he's your dog," I shout after her.

I turn back to the door in time to see Aspen and Lyric stroll into the house. "Does no one know how to knock in this town?"

Aspen's brow wrinkles. "Why would we knock? You invited us over."

I move away from Rowan to take the crockpot out of her hands. "You should still knock."

"And miss the chance to embarrass you when we barge in on you and Rowan having sexy times?"

I groan. "You remind me of Mom."

"Who reminds you of me?" Mom asks as she too walks straight into the house without knocking with Dad trailing after her.

"Are we referring to personality or outer appearance?" Lilac asks as she arrives with Ellery.

"Watch out! Lilac the sociologist is in the house," Aspen says as she grabs a plate and digs into my seven-layer dip.

"Finally," Rowan mumbles before shoveling half of the dip onto his plate together with a mound of chips.

"I made the dip for our guests, too," I tell him.

He shrugs before joining Lyric and Dad on the sofa.

"Okay." Bryan nods toward me. "We've got rid of the men. Now, tell us all about how Rowan is in the sack."

Ellery pretends to gag. "Veto!"

"What are we vetoing?" Lyric's brother, River, asks as he enters the house.

I ignore him to grab the plate his brother, Phoenix, is carrying. "Yes!" I cry when I notice the assortment of cheeses on the platter.

"Five minutes," Rowan barks a warning.

Bryan's lips purse. "Uh oh. He used his football voice."

"His football voice?" I ask.

"Mm-hmm. It's his serious voice, but since it only comes out during football, I refer to it as his football voice."

I waggle my eyebrows at him. "I don't know. I think I may have heard the voice at other times."

He throws an arm around my shoulders and leads me toward the living room. "I believe this is the beginning of a beautiful friendship."

When we near the sofa, Rowan snags my hand and pulls me down to sit next to him. After I settle in with him, I survey the room with my friends and family in attendance. This, right here, is the dream.

I catch Mom's eyes and she smiles at me. *I love you, baby girl,* she mouths. And, for once, the baby reference doesn't annoy me.

Rowan kisses my hair. "The dip was worth waiting for."

You were worth waiting for, I think but don't say. I'm not about to get all sappy about finally having Rowan where I've wanted him for-freaking-ever in front of my family who will have no qualms about teasing me for the rest of my life about getting all sentimental while watching a football game.

"Who wants to make a friendly wager about the game?" Lilac asks.

"Girl," Bryan tuts and wags a finger at her, "there are no 'friendly' wagers when it comes to Rowan Aries Hansley and the National Football League."

"True." Lyric nods. "Rowan is a sore loser."

Rowan growls. "I am not a sore loser. You're a cheater."

Lyric rolls his eyes. "I did not steal your lucky socks."

I lean back to meet Rowan's gaze. "Lucky socks? I didn't know you were superstitious."

"All professional football players are superstitious," Bryan answers. "And let me tell you, the only thing not washing a jockstrap is going to bring you is jock itch. Not good luck."

"Gross." Ellery feigns throwing up except she does genuinely appear ill.

"Please tell me you washed your jockstrap."

Rowan ignores me to tell Lyric, "I know you stole my lucky socks. River ratted you out."

When Lyric glares at his brother, River's eyes widen, and he starts edging toward the door. Behind me, Rowan growls.

"You lied," he accuses.

Phoenix hurries to stand in front of River. "It's been more than a decade. There's no reason to pound River's head into the floor for a prank he played when he was a teenager."

"Thanks for giving him the idea," River mutters from behind him.

"Prank? We lost the championship," Rowan grumbles and starts to stand.

I jump on his lap to stop him from moving. "No bloodshed on game day. I don't clean bloodstains."

"Another thing she doesn't clean," Juniper mutters. "You should probably hire a maid before it's too late."

I glare at her. Rowan and I haven't agreed to live together yet. She knows I'm worried about what's going to happen when my boot comes off. Does he expect me to move home? It's awful early to live together, but we've spent every night together since Sandra left town a few days ago.

"Give it a rest," Lyric says and brings me out of my reverie. "You won enough championships playing college ball and you have a Super Bowl ring. What difference does it make now anyway?"

"I don't know why everyone's getting their panties in a twist," Bryan argues as he watches the drama.

As one, the men rivet their attention on him and shout, "It's football!"

"In case anyone cares, it's kick-off," Lilac announces.

She said the magic words. The testosterone in the room drops and the men settle back into their seats to watch the game.

"They stop the clock an awful lot," Mom says a few minutes later, and Dad grunts in agreement. He's a football fan. As in the 'real' football the whole world plays. I've tried to tell him the world plays soccer, but he refuses to listen.

Bryan groans. "No. Stop. No talk of the clock. I can't bear it."

"Clock management is an essential element of offensive team tactics," Rowan says.

"Uh oh. He's gearing up for a lecture." Bryan sighs and stands. "Who wants another drink?"

"Do you not like football?" I ask him.

He shrugs. "It's okay, I guess."

My brow wrinkles in confusion. "But weren't you Rowan's personal assistant when he played professionally?"

"And a damn fine assistant I was, too."

My gaze whips back and forth between Rowan and Bryan. "I'm confused."

Rowan grunts.

"Saying it's not a big deal isn't an explanation," I tell him.

"Good luck there, girlie," Bryan chuckles. "Someone believes grunting is an answer to every question in existence."

"I'm serious." I pinch Rowan's side. "Why did you hire Bryan to be your PA if he doesn't like football?"

He leans down to whisper in my ear. "Because he's my friend and I trust him."

I melt him to him. "You're a good man, Rowan Aries."

"My job here is finished," Aspen declares with a big 'ol smile on her face.

Her job? She's not the one who worked through Rowan's issues about making a woman happy with him. Not unless— No! I refuse to believe it. There's no way Aspen contacted Sandra and asked her to come to town. She wouldn't be so cruel.

Only when I notice the out of this word smirk on my big sister's face, I'm not as sure. I narrow my eyes at her, and she flutters her lashes like some innocent young thing. Innocent my ass.

Chapter 30

Lightweight – a person who doesn't need to spend much money before a good time finds her

Rowan grabs my hand before I can jump out of the golf cart. "Have fun tonight."

I beam at him. "I will."

"And be safe."

I roll my eyes. "Be safe? We're in Winter Falls. What possible danger could there be?" For good measure, I flutter my eyelashes at him.

He groans. "At least don't resist arrest."

I clutch my chest and widen my eyes. "As if I would dare."

He tugs on my hand until I'm practically laying across his lap. "Don't think I'm unaware you've been behaving because of your ankle," he whispers against my lips before softly sipping from them.

I sigh and debate ordering him to turn the golf cart around and take me home.

"Ashlyn Dream!" Juniper shouts. "Keep your pants on. No one wants to see your pale butt."

"As if I'd ever have a pale butt!" I shout back.

Rowan lifts me off of his lap and sets me on the ground. "Be good."

"Where is everyone?" I ask when I enter *Fall Into A Good Book*. I scan the room, but the only people here thus far are my sisters, but I know for a fact Feather, Petal, Sage, Cayenne, and Clove signed up for the paint and sip evening.

"I thought we'd update everyone on the mystery first," Aspen answers.

I march to the door and lock it. "Is the backdoor locked?"

Aspen rolls her eyes. "Do I look like an amateur?"

"Amateur in what?" Lilac asks and Aspen hisses at her. "What? You can't ask a question without defining the parameters. How am I supposed to answer?"

"It was a rhetorical question. A rhetorical question is—," I begin, but Lilac interrupts me before I can define it for her.

"I know what a rhetorical question is. I think it's use—"

I shove my hand in her face before she can continue. No one wants to hear a lecture from Ms. Know It All on English grammar. Trust me. I've heard the lecture. Thirty minutes of my life I will never get back.

"We know where the loot is!" Aspen bursts out.

"What? Where? How did you figure it out?" Juniper asks.

"We went to visit Old Man Mercury," I begin before explaining how we learned about the *Winter Creek Bulletin* and found the clue buried there.

There may be some rubbing it in Lilac's face about how I knew something before she did. It's not every day I get the chance to tell my older sister I got the drop on her. I'd lose my little sister badge if I neglected to rub it in.

"Which is how we know the loot is buried by the cornerstone at the inn," I conclude.

Ellery crosses her arms over her chest. "No."

"No what?"

"No, you aren't going to dig up the front lawn of the inn. I won't allow it."

"Come on," I cajole. "Don't be a wet blanket."

"I'm not a wet blanket. I'm a business owner who spent more money than you will earn in your lifetime renovating the old mansion. I will not allow you to destroy all my hard work."

"Harsh. You don't even know how much money I make."

"Plus, she's shacked up with a millionaire now," Juniper points out.

I glare at her. "We're not shacked up."

"You appeared awful comfortable on Sunday." She lifts an eyebrow in an obvious effort to force me to deny it, and I – being the mature adult I am – stick my tongue out at her.

Before we can continue, there's a knock on the door. "Soleil's here," Aspen announces. "We'll continue this discussion later."

Or I'll just find a shovel and dig in the inn's yard without anyone being the wiser. Either way works for me.

Aspen unlocks the door for Soleil. Soleil's an artistic jack of all trades. She does pottery and teaches pottery classes, she knits and sells her 'inventions' on Esty, and she paints. Tonight, she's leading our paint and sip evening.

"I'll help with the wine," I announce before heading to the checkout counter where Aspen has several bottles laid out, opening the first one, and taking a large gulp straight from the bottle.

"You are so uncouth," Ellery frowns at me.

I offer her the bottle. "You want some?"

She leans away from me. "No, thanks."

"Your loss," I say.

"Don't hog the bottle." Juniper snatches the bottle with such a vengeance from me I nearly fall down.

"There are glasses, you know," Aspen says and hands me one.

The bell over the door rings and Feather, Petal, Sage, Cayenne, and Clove traipse into the bookstore.

Petal scans the room in confusion. "Where's Rowan?"

"At home," I tell her. "Where else would he be?" She doesn't seriously think Rowan would attend an event at the bookstore, does she?

"I assumed he was our model for the evening," she answers and the other ladies sigh. "If he isn't going to model, we'll have to settle for you giving us all the details."

"Yes, Ashlyn, we want all the details," Bryan adds as he joins us.

"You must have seen him naked before."

He licks his lips. "Oh, I have. But I've never seen him naked and in action, if you know what I mean." He waggles his eyebrows and I feel my face – as well as other body parts – warm.

"Girlie," he says and points to my face, "I have to know what has you sporting the dreamy look."

He crowds around me with the other ladies, but I hold up my hands. "No way. You know how Rowan is about his privacy."

Bryan sticks out his bottom lip and pouts. "I do, but I hoped you didn't."

Seriously? How could I not know he's fanatic about his privacy? No one besides me – and I assume, Bryan – even knows how his marriage ended. Everyone assumes Sandra the Gold Digger cheated on him, and Rowan lets them think what they want. He never corrects anyone's assumptions.

Aspen pushes her way through everyone to stand next to me. "Ladies, we're here to paint and sip, not gossip."

Sage laughs. "Sometimes I find it hard to believe you grew up here, Aspen Cloud. It's almost as if you've forgotten the ways of Winter Falls."

I mouth *thank you* to Aspen before rushing off to find a place to sit. It's not hiding when there's a canvas in front of you.

"Tonight, we'll be painting an orchid," Soleil begins before explaining some painting techniques to us.

An hour later, Gracious arrives with several bags of food. The scent of pizza, burgers, and fries emanates from the bags the diner owner brought. Yum. When I stand to get some food, I wobble. I have to clutch the back of the chair to steady myself.

"And now you know why I asked Gracious to bring food," Aspen frowns as she watches me.

"What? You're the one who organized a paint and sip night. I'm following your directions. I'm painting and sipping."

There may be a bit more sipping than painting going on, but no one said the two must be done equally.

"Whatever."

I follow her to the counter where the food is being laid out. As I stroll through the room, I check out the other paintings. I screech to a halt when I notice someone thought this was male anatomy night. "Holy cow! Who painted the penis?"

Bryan raises his hand. "It's good, isn't it?"

I step closer. "Is it a self-portrait?"

Everyone gathers around me to study the painting.

"It's really big. My Orion isn't this big," Petal says.

"I don't think it's life-sized," I say.

"Oh." She frowns.

"It's very symmetrical. Sirius's balls are uneven. It's never bothered me, but I can't help but notice," Clove tells us. "Plus, it bothers him. He never wants me to touch the smaller one. I feel bad for it."

I giggle. "You feel bad for your husband's balls?"

"One of my breasts is smaller than the other one," Cayenne announces. "Arlo never seemed to mind. He gave it extra attention if you know what I mean."

Arlo is Cayenne's deceased husband. I never met him as he passed before I was born.

"I've never been with a woman," Bryan announces. "Does it matter if the breasts are asymmetrical? Is this a thing?"

Cayenne tugs on her shirt and I grab her hand. "No. It's not show and tell time."

"Bryan doesn't care."

He nods. "It's intellectual curiosity."

Lilac sighs. "Why do people say 'intellectual curiosity' when they actually mean they're being nosy? Intellectual curiosity is about acquiring knowledge, not about comparing the size of someone's right breast to her left. Breast asymmetry affects more than half of women. There, your 'intellectual curiosity' has been satisfied."

Normally, I'd be annoyed with Lilac's wet blanket comment, but she has efficiently stopped show and tell hour and I'm thankful to her. We'd start with viewing Cayenne's breasts, but who knows where it would end?

Cayenne tucks her blouse back in and everyone returns to their original activity – eating the yummy snacks Gracious brought us. An hour later, we pack up. I'm fairly satisfied with my painting. Maybe I'll hang it in my bedroom back home.

"Where to now?" Juniper asks as we leave the bookstore with our paintings in hand.

"I need to get back to the inn," Ellery says and marches off without waiting for a reply.

"I have an early meeting tomorrow," Lilac announces before following Ellery.

"And I'm off to wake my husband to ravish him," Aspen announces.

Juniper wrinkles her nose at me. "I suppose you're off to ravish Rowan as well."

I lace my arm through hers. "Nope. He'll be fast asleep since he needs to start baking at a time when no one in the world who's sober should be awake. I can't complain, though, his pastries are utterly delicious." Although, his sleep schedule is going to take some getting used to.

"Awesome. The brewery's still open."

Aspen moans. "Please tell me you won't get in trouble. It'd be nice if my husband could have an uninterrupted night of sleep for once."

I snort. "One, he's not your husband yet. Two, you're the one who just said you're going home to wake Lyric up. And last but not least, the fight wasn't our fault."

She crosses her arms over her chest and lifts her eyebrow. "Not your fault? You literally called the guy a piece of scum not worthy of being attached to your shoe before you throat punched him."

She's not lying, but, "You're taking my words out of context."

She throws her hands up in the air. "I can't. I just can't with you."

I wave as she leaves. "Have fun!"

"You good to walk?" Juniper asks as we set off in the direction of the brewery.

"I am feeling no pain, sis. No pain at all."

She giggles. "How much wine did you drink?"

"Moon's working tonight," I say instead of answering her since I have no idea how much I drank. "I bet she'll sneak us some food."

I begin skipping toward the brewery but skipping with a walking cast is not a good idea. I settle for dancing my way down the street instead. I feel wonderful. Rowan is in bed at home waiting for me to return. My cast comes off soon. And I landed a new narration assignment today. Can life get any better?

Chapter 31

Light the lamp – to score a goal in the sexiest way possible

ROWAN

I roll over and check the clock once again. Ten o'clock. Usually, I'm asleep by nine on nights before I need to open the bakery the next morning, but I'm finding sleep difficult to find tonight. It's the first night I haven't slept with Ash beside me and I'm not too much of a man to admit I miss her warm body cuddled up to mine.

I was an idiot to avoid her for the past year. I could have been sleeping next to her for months instead of weeks. But I'm not going to dwell on my mistake and ruin my future. It's in the past. Rowan the Idiot has left the building.

I flop onto my back and consider messaging Ash to make sure she's okay. Who am I kidding? If anything happens to her, I'll know within minutes especially considering the Gossip Gals are attending the paint and sip evening at Aspen's bookstore.

I must manage to fall asleep because the next time I check the clock it's midnight. Where is she? She said they'd be finished by ten. I'm halfway out of bed when I hear the front door open. An object falls to the floor and Ash swears.

"Stay there," she mumbles.

Stay there? Did she bring someone home with her? What the hell? I switch on the light but before I can roll out of bed to confront her, she stumbles into the room and collides with the foot of the bedframe.

"Are you okay?"

"I'm fine," she shouts from where she landed on the floor.

"Did you bring someone home with you?"

She peeks over the bed frame and blinks up at me. "Who would I have brought home? I promise there's not a goat in your living room."

Shit. There's a goat in my living room. I fling the covers off of me and stand. Ash wraps her arms around my leg before I can move.

"Really." She giggles. "There are no goats in your living room. Or a lynx or a caribou or a porcupine."

I rub a hand over my face before reaching down to pick Ash up and lay her on the bed. I come down on top of her.

"What are you talking about?"

Her fingers trace around the lines in my forehead before gliding down my nose and across my cheeks. "Your face is far too pretty for a man. It's not fair." She pinches my lips together. "And your lips are way softer than any other man's."

I ignore the little ball of jealousy in my stomach at her reference to other men's lips she's kissed. She won't be kissing anyone other than me from now on. The thought is enough to dispel any remnants of envy.

Her nails scratch my jaw. "Why don't you have a beard now? You always had one when you played football."

"You want me to grow a beard, I'll grow a beard."

She glances away and since we're close, I can feel the heat emanate from her cheeks. I grin. "Do you want to know how it feels to have my face between your legs when I have a beard?"

She nods and I lean my forehead against hers. "Okay. I'll grow a beard."

"Just like that?"

"It isn't hard."

She wiggles beneath me. "But I do feel something that is hard."

I pump my hips into her stomach, and she arches her back until her chest is rubbing against mine. "What are we going to do about it?"

"I'm going to ravish you."

I chuckle. "Aren't I the one who's supposed to ravish you?"

"Nope. It's my turn." She wraps a leg around me and twists until I'm lying on my back and she's looming over me.

I realize there's something missing. "Where's your boot?"

"I took it off in the living room."

She grinds down on me before I can remind her she needs to wear her boot all the time unless she's in the shower.

I fist her hair and use the hold to bring her to me. "How much have you had to drink?" I ask against her lips.

"More than a little. Less than a lot."

"Am I going to get a visit from Chief Alston tomorrow?" I tease. She hums and tries to twist out of my hold. Shit. I was only joking. "Ash?"

She shrugs. "No one saw us."

"Saw you what?"

"It's Juniper's fault."

"What's Juniper's fault?"

"Everything?"

"Nice try. What did you do?"

"It's not a big deal." I wait her out. "Can we move along to the sexy times now?"

"As soon as you tell me what you did and reassure me I won't be visiting you in jail for the next five to ten years."

"Fine," she huffs. "We made an altar to a skunk in River's front yard. It's his own dang fault. He never should have stolen your lucky socks."

I release her hair to wrap my arms around her as I burst out laughing. "You made an altar for a skunk? Please tell me you didn't kill a skunk."

"It's a stuffed animal and there are little sacrifices to the dearly departed little guy. It's some of my best work."

"You know how much River's scared of skunks after the time he accidentally got stuck in the locker room with one. Man, it took us months to get rid of the smell. He can't even watch Pepé Le Pew on television without freaking out."

She giggles. "Why do you think we picked a skunk?"

"I hope no one saw you."

"We're only honoring the memory of poor Sami, officer." She flutters her eyelashes.

"You're crazy, dream girl."

When I say dream girl, her face softens and her body melts into mine. "I love you, Rowan." I open my mouth to respond, but she doesn't give me the chance. "Now, ravish me."

My lips find hers. I intend to go gentle, but she bites my bottom lip, and my intentions fly out the window. I tangle my hands in her hair and tilt her head until I can explore every inch of her mouth. Her sunshine and chocolate flavor hit my tongue and I moan.

She shivers at the sound and then her hands begin roaming my chest. When she reaches my waist, she shoves her hands under my t-shirt and bunches the fabric upward until I'm forced to lose her mouth in order for her to divest me of my shirt.

"Finally." She sighs as she sits up while her fingers trail patterns on my bare skin.

"Two can play at this game," I tell her.

Before I can make my move, she rips her top off to reveal her lacy bra.

"I'm winning," she cries.

My hands find her lace-covered breasts. I squeeze and her head falls back as she groans.

"Who's winning now?"

"Pretty sure, it's still me," she pants out as she thrusts her chest into my hands.

I jackknife up until my mouth is close enough to bite her nipple through the lace. In response, she grinds down on my erection. Oh yeah, we're both winning.

I reach around and unfasten her bra before flinging the lace across the room. My mouth returns to devouring her breast. While my teeth play with the silky smooth skin, my hand massages her other breast.

Suddenly, I lose her. She rolls off me and lays on her back as she pushes her jeans and underwear down her legs.

"In a hurry?" I ask.

"You're the one with the monster erection."

"Monster? Why, thank you."

She slaps my bare chest. "Don't get conceited. I saw an even bigger penis today."

The words are barely out of her mouth before I'm crawling on top of her to cage her in. "Whose penis did you see?"

"I don't know."

I growl. "You don't know? How can you not know?"

"Bryan wouldn't tell us who it belonged to. All I know is it wasn't his."

"What are you talking about?"

She giggles. "Paint and sip class. Bryan painted a huge penis. The balls were incredibly symmetrical."

I thrust my hard length against her. "Are you saying my balls are uneven?"

"I don't know. I think I need to do further research first." She wiggles her eyebrows. "Get rid of your pants and we can begin."

I grin as I roll to my back to discard my pajama bottoms. They're still around my ankles when Ash attacks. She leaps on top of me and starts rubbing her slit over my hard length. I clench my jaw to stop myself from grabbing her hips and sliding in.

"Shit. Ash. This is going to be over before it can begin if you don't stop."

She stills. "Are you telling me Rowan the football god has a problem with premature ejaculation?"

I dig my fingers into her hips. "I think you know by now I don't have a problem with premature anything," I grumble.

She cocks a brow. "Oh yeah? Let's prove it."

Before I can respond, she fists my cock and hovers her core above it. She pauses for a second to wink at me before slamming herself down on me.

I groan and my fingers tighten on her hips. "You're killing me, dream girl."

"Ah, but what a way to go." She lifts up before gliding back down on my cock.

My balls feel heavy and there's already a tingle in my spine. Holy hell. The woman is seriously going to be the death of me.

"Slow down," I demand.

"Make me," she moans as she tightens her inner muscles around my cock.

"You asked for it," I growl before I lift her off my cock. I punch my hips up as I slam her down.

She gasps before demanding, "Do it again."

Her command is my wish. She arches her back and rests her hands on my thighs for balance as I lift her up and down on my cock. It's not long before her fingernails are boring into my skin. I'm going to have little half-moon bruises on my thighs, and I don't care one bit.

"Reach between your legs and play with yourself, Ash," I demand between thrusts.

She lifts her gaze until she's eye to eye with me. She stares into my eyes as her hand drifts down her body to where we're joined. She flicks her clit once, twice…

"I'm going to," she gasps out.

"Do it, dream girl. Come for me."

She tightens around me, and I lose her eyes when her back bows. "Rowan," she rasps.

"Right here, Ash. I'm right here."

My thrusts become erratic as her orgasm sets mine off. I continue to pump into her as I slowly come down from my climax.

Ash collapses against my chest. "Life can get better," she whispers before promptly passing out.

I don't know what she's talking about, but I have to disagree with her. It doesn't get any better than Ash naked in my bed after the best sex of my life.

Chapter 32

Par for the course – what's expected except what one person expects isn't necessarily what the other does

I SMILE AS I burrow into the warm body behind me. Wait. Warm body? Rowan's home? I glance at the clock. It's nearly nine. He should be at the bakery.

His arm tightens around my waist and mutters, "Sleep."

I elbow him. "Rowan, you need to get up. The bakery."

"The bakery's fine."

"I'm serious, honey. It's almost nine o'clock. The natives are probably getting restless. They'll arrive with pitchforks in your yard any moment now."

"Pitchforks? This town doesn't use violence to solve its problems. They'll stage a strike or a sit-in or some other form of non-violent protest."

"I don't think..." My words drop off as I realize this conversation is pointless. "Why are we discussing this? You need to move."

He kisses my neck and cuddles in closer. "I already got up and did the majority of the baking."

"You did? How did I not hear you getting out of bed?"

"You heard me. You said, and I quote here, 'use the servant entrance, the dark lord is waiting for you in the turret'."

I groan. I blame the fantasy romance I'm narrating for the weird dreams, although the sexy ones are all Rowan. The man knows how to use his body. Lucky me.

I wiggle my ass against his groin, and he growls. "I thought you wanted to sleep," he grumbles.

"Sleep? Who said anything about sleep?"

His arm around my waist lifts until his hand covers my breast and he squeezes. I moan and arch my back.

"I like where this is going," I manage to wheeze out.

I was wrong. I didn't like where it was going. I freaking loved it. I grin as I allow the water in the shower to flow down my back. A knock raps on the shower door and startles me.

"No dilly-dallying. We have places to be," Rowan yells through the door.

"We do?" I ask, but he's already gone. He's being mysterious. Yes! I love it.

I rush through getting ready. I throw on some jeans and a sweater before putting my wet hair into a messy bun. I don't bother with make-up. I hardly ever bother with the stuff, to be honest.

I clomp to the kitchen and skid to a stop when I notice Rowan standing there drinking coffee and staring out the window to the backyard. His house is on the street furthest from Main Street meaning there are no other houses behind his – just woods and a trail leading to the river and the falls.

I wrap my arms around him from behind. "It's peaceful here."

He nods. "It is. I dreamed of Winter Falls when I was playing football. All those travel days, sleeping in hotels in cities where the traffic would keep me awake at night." He sighs. "I couldn't wait to get back home."

I lean my cheek against his back. "Really? I thought you were devastated about your injury when you came back," I say and hold my breath. Rowan never talks about his injury. I hope I'm not stepping onto a landmine here, especially since I only have one good leg at the moment.

He squeezes my arm. "Don't get me wrong. My injury was devastating."

"I'm sorry," I whisper.

He unwinds my arms and turns around to face me. "Don't be sorry. It wasn't your fault. Am I disappointed my career ended abruptly at the age of twenty-nine? Of course, I am. But I'm over it. I had seven years of playing professional football. It's more than most boys who dream of being in the NFL will ever have."

I tilt my head back to gaze into his eyes. "You're over it?"

He bops my nose. "I am. I have a great business. I have wonderful friends. I have this kooky town. And now I have you."

I beam up at him. "You sure do."

He leans over to touch my lips in the briefest of kisses. I mewl in protest when he pulls away and he chuckles. "We're on a schedule."

"We are? Where are we going?" I ask as my stomach rumbles.

"First, to feed the monster inside you."

I regard the kitchen counters. Empty. "No pancakes," I pout.

"Spoiled brat."

He herds me toward the golf cart. "I can walk," I protest.

He stops to frown down at me. "The same way you walked around all last night?"

I cock an eyebrow. "How do you know I didn't bike or ride a golf cart?"

He pinches my chin. "Because I saw how swollen your ankle was this morning. I can spot an overuse injury a mile away."

Damnit. I had to fall in love with a former professional athlete. "Fine." I give in.

We climb into the golf cart. "To breakfast, Jeeves!"

We pass *Bake Me Happy* and continue toward the diner. "You sure about this," I ask as he grasps my hand to lead me inside. "The Gossip Gals as you lovingly refer to Feather, Petal, Sage, Cayenne, and Clove is going to attack the minute we enter the diner holding hands."

"Nice try. We're not returning home, so I can make you pancakes."

Dang. He saw right through me. "Fine," I huff.

Gracious rushes to us the minute the door opens. "Rowan! Ashlyn! I have your table ready."

Table ready? The diner doesn't accept reservations. It's first come, first serve. She motions us to the booth furthest away from the door along the window.

As we make our way to the booth, I watch as everyone in the place types on their phone. I'm sure money exchanges hands as well, but I don't see it.

"French toast and a big coffee for Ash," Gracious announces as we sit. "And oatmeal with a side of sausage for Rowan." She leaves before we can respond to her orders for us.

I lean over the booth and whisper, "What do you want to bet everyone's on the Facebook page announcing a sighting of Ashwan?"

"Ashwan?" He chuckles.

"Ashlyn and Rowan. Duh."

"First, I'm vetoing that portmanteau. It sounds similar to a curse word in a foreign language."

I clap my hands. "Which is why I love it!"

Rowan ignores me. "Second, I will never bet against the town being a bunch of snoops."

"Excuse me," Sage hisses from the booth behind him. "I prefer the term busybody."

I giggle. Only a resident of Winter Falls would think the term busybody is a badge of honor.

"What's the plan for today?" I ask Rowan after our coffee arrives.

He cocks a brow. "Plan?"

"You said we have places to be. Places. Plural."

He smirks. "I'd rather show than tell."

Sage harrumphs from behind him and he winks.

Our food arrives and I dig into my French toast. I point to his oatmeal with my fork. "Oatmeal seems an odd choice for a baker."

He shrugs. "I don't train the way I used to. I can't afford to eat empty calories anymore."

"And I can?"

"I think you're perfectly aware of how much I enjoy your body, dream girl."

Sage sighs. "How much does he love your body, Ashlyn? Details please."

I growl. Can't she tell I'm trying to have a moment with my man here? "Aren't you needed at the police station?"

"Lyric can get along fine without me."

"I can?" Lyric asks as he comes to stand next to her table.

"Oh dear. My break must be over," Sage proclaims as she slides out of her booth and rushes out of the diner.

Lyric shakes his head. "The bane of my existence."

"Good morning, future brother-in-law."

"Good morning, bane of my existence number two."

I widen my eyes and flutter my lashes. "Whatever do you mean, Chief?"

He crosses his arms over his chest. "Really? This is how you're going to play it?"

I drop my innocent act. "I have no idea what you're talking about, Officer."

He snorts. "How many times have you said those words, Ashlyn?"

I wrinkle my nose. "Once?"

"You're such a liar," he says but there's no heat in his words. "Did you have fun last night?"

"The paint and sip event your future wife organized was a blast." I deliberately misconstrue his words.

"Too bad I couldn't enjoy my tipsy fiancée when she came home as I got summoned for a disturbance."

He did? We didn't disturb anyone. River was fast asleep when we left. Across from me, Rowan groans. Idiot. He should know better than to make any admissions of guilt. And, yes, a groan can be construed as an admission of guilt. You quickly learn this when the police always confront you first whenever anything happens.

"River was pissed. And refused to leave the safety of his home because of the 'skunk' in his front yard." Lyric winks.

"He probably shouldn't steal socks then."

Lyric clasps Rowan on the shoulder. "You got your hands full with this one."

"But what fun it is," I sing as Lyric departs while shaking his head.

"See? There's no reason to visit your girlfriend in the clink."

Rowan barks out a laugh and I enjoy the show. His brown eyes sparkle, and the muscles in his neck contract as he tilts his head back. When his laughter dies, he taps my plate with his fork. "Finish your food. We have places to be."

"Told you, places was plural," I say before doing as I'm told.

Once we finish our late breakfast, we hop in the golf cart once again. "Where are we going now, Jeeves?"

"What's with the Jeeves references?"

My eyes widen in surprise. "You don't know who Jeeves is? I don't know if we can be special friends anymore."

"Oh, we're going to be special friends," he promises in his deep, growly voice, and all the fun places on my body tingle in response. "And I know who Jeeves is. What I don't know is why you're obsessed with the butler."

I clutch my non-existent pearls. "Jeeves is not a butler. He's a valet."

"I thought your sister Aspen was the book nerd."

I snort. "She is. She really is." I clear my throat before explaining. "There's a play, *Jeeves and Wooster in Perfect Nonsense*, based on one of P.G. Woodhouse's novels. It's a three-man play, but when I was in college, we decided to make it a three-woman play. I played Bertie, who is a big noob if you ask me."

Rowan squeezes my hand. "I bet you were wonderful."

I roll my eyes. "Which is why I'm now narrating audiobooks instead of acting on Broadway."

He pulls the golf cart to stop and turns to give me his full attention. "Is acting on Broadway your dream?"

I frown and shrug. "I don't know. I thought it was." My old and familiar insecurities about failing rear their ugly heads. "But I wasn't good enough anyway."

He lifts my hand to his lips and kisses my fingers. "Ash, you are good enough."

"How would you know?"

"You were the lead in every play the Winter Falls High School ever put on."

"Being the lead in a town of a thousand people doesn't scream talent."

"What about all the plays you starred in while in college?"

My brow wrinkles. "How would you know if I starred in any plays in college?"

"Ash, Ash, Ash," he tsks. "This town is proud of you. The moment you were chosen for a new play, the information spread faster than wildfire."

I shrug. "It was only college."

He pinches my chin before I can avert my gaze. "Only college? You mean the college that specialized in drama where graduates often ended up on Broadway or as Hollywood stars?"

"Not everyone who graduated became a star," I mumble.

His gaze becomes laser focused on me, and I lock my muscles to stop myself from squirming.

"What are you afraid of?"

My back straightens, and I pull away from him. "I'm not afraid of anything."

Nope. I'm afraid of everything. Not everything, but the most important thing there is – failing. I was fine when I was in college due to my competitive spirit. You can't grow up the youngest of five sisters and not end up competitive. But when I graduated and realized there were dozens of colleges with graduates who thought they had the chops to make it on Broadway, my fear took over and I retreated.

"Okay. I get it now," he says as he steps out of the cart.

"What do you get?" I shout after him.

"You'll see." Before I can remind him I don't think much of his non-answer, he continues. "We're here."

"Here?" I search the area. "The brewery isn't open yet."

"It is for us."

Now, I'm intrigued. "What's going on?"

He shrugs and places his hands in his pockets. "I thought you might enjoy a taste test of the new autumn IPAs from *Naked Falls Brewing*."

I leap out of the cart. "What are you waiting for? Let's go."

Our conversation about how I'm inadequate and afraid of failing is immediately forgotten as I make my way to the front door. Mistake. I should have remembered.

Chapter 33

Ringer – someone who knows the loophole to win the game and doesn't hesitate to use it

ROWAN

I stand with my arms crossed over my chest in front of the door blocking Ash's exit from the house. "You're not going."

She waves a hand in dismissal. "Sure, I am. It's for charity."

"I don't care if it's for the Queen of fucking England. You are not going."

She giggles. "I don't think there's a Queen of Fucking England. Where is this kingdom? Next to Screwing Scotland?"

"Don't be cute." She beams at me. "You are not doing a fun run with a broken ankle."

She lifts her boot. "I have a walking cast."

"And I was there the days after you decided to wander around all night after paint and sip. I saw how much pain you were in. Not again."

Every time she winced, I had to beat back the impulse to wrap her in cotton and secure her in our house until her bones healed. At least I managed to force her to take a few baths to help with the swelling, although she only conceded after I agreed to join her. It wasn't a hardship.

"You're not going to give on this? I can't walk the poker run?"

I nod. "Correct."

She claps. "I guess you'll have to push me then."

I cock an eyebrow. "Push you?"

"In a wheelchair," she says.

"What wheelchair?"

"The one I borrowed from Dr. Blue's office because I knew you'd go ballistic if I tried to walk the poker run."

"If you knew I'd go ballistic, why did you fight with me?"

She grins. "Because it's fun to watch the vein in your forehead pulse." I grit my teeth. She's driving me crazy. "And there goes the muscle twitching in your jaw."

"You enjoy making me mad."

"Damn straight. You are sexy on a normal day. But when you're mad?" She fans her face. "You are f-i-n-e. Fine."

I step toward her and place a hand on her hip. "We can skip the poker run." I slide my hand from her hip to her ass and squeeze in case there's any uncertainty about what we would be doing instead.

She kisses my jaw before stepping away. "Raincheck! I have a poker run record to keep."

The poker run is a big annual charity event in Winter Falls. It attracts tourists from all over as the grand prize for having the best poker hand is an all-inclusive week at the *Inn on Main*.

The worst hand wins dinner at the *Naked Falls Brewing* brewery including a sampler package of their beers.

There are also prizes donated by local businesses at each stop such as a basket of treats from the bakery and a necklace from *Bohemian Treasures*. All proceeds from entry fees and food and consumptions are donated to the chosen charity. This year's charity is the community center. Or, I should say, the future community center as there isn't one currently.

"A poker run record?" I ask, but Ash is already out the door.

I follow and find her sitting in a wheelchair. I half believed she lied about the chair, but since she didn't, I can hardly deny her wish to participate. Damnit.

She lifts her hand and points toward the town center. "To the start, Jeeves!"

"Let's discuss strategy," she says as I begin pushing her.

"Strategy? It's poker. It's a game of chance."

She sighs and tuts. "Rowan. Rowan. Rowan. You don't understand. I will have the best poker hand at the end."

"You're not going to cheat, are you?" I wouldn't put it past her. "Should I have frisked you for a deck of cards before we left?"

She tips her head back to smirk at me. "You can frisk me any time, big boy. But you know the committee uses unique decks of cards for the event."

"Isn't your sister in charge?"

She crosses her arms over her chest and huffs. "Is she really a sister if she refuses to provide me with advance information about the decks of cards being used?"

"Maybe she's not a cheater."

"I say wet blanket, you say not a cheater. Tomato. Tomahto."

"You're trouble," I tell her.

"I think you have the word trouble confused with fun."

We arrive at the town square to find the entire population of Winter Falls milling around. The crowd is thick as there are loads of tourists as well.

I wave to Bryan at the *Bake Me Happy* booth. He notices me and scowls in my direction.

"Is this how it's going to be now you've got a woman?" he shouts at me. "I'm stuck doing all the work."

"Need I remind you of the past two years when I ran the booth because you hooked up with some tourist?"

"Worth it," he squeals.

"Don't worry," Ash tells him. "Next year, I'll have both legs at my disposal, and he can go back to manning the booth."

Next year? My chest warms at the idea of all the years Ash and I have in our future. We may have lost one to my being a fool, but we have our entire lives to make up for the lost time.

"Five-minute warning," Forest announces over the megaphone.

"We need to get to our starting position," Ash urges me.

"Where do you want to begin?"

She indicates the furthest corner of the square where the crowd is thinner.

"There are seven checkpoints, and you have to visit five," she explains. "But, here's the rule no one knows about, you are allowed to visit seven. You can then choose your five best cards."

Suddenly, I understand why Ash is the poker run champion. "Let me guess. No one else knows about the rule?"

She winks up at me. "Nope. Except Lilac, but she tells everyone to read the rules when they ask her questions. I can't help it if no one else bothered to read them."

"What about the rest of your sisters? Didn't you tell them about this loophole?"

"It's not a loophole," she claims. "But it doesn't matter. None of them participate anyway. Juniper won't leave her precious animals at the wildlife refuge. Lilac can't participate as it's a conflict of interest." She makes a face as if a conflict of interest is the most boring thing in the world. "Ellery has to man the inn and Aspen has a booth."

"But what do you do with the all-inclusive week at the inn if you win?" I probably should say when at this point.

"I donate it," she mumbles.

"What did you say?"

"I donate it, okay? There's a women's shelter near the hospital and I give it to them for one of the women to have a treat."

"Why do you sound embarrassed?" She won't meet my gaze, so I kneel in front of her until we're eye to eye. "Hey. Being generous is nothing to be embarrassed about."

"I'm not embarrassed, but you have to admit it would ruin my reputation as a troublemaker."

I chuckle before standing to kiss her forehead. "Don't worry. Nothing's going to ruin your reputation as a troublemaker."

"Let the countdown begin!" Forest shouts. "Ten, nine, eight, seven, six, five, four, three, two, one. Go!!"

Before I can begin pushing Ash, she's using her hands to power her away to the first station. "Come on, slowpoke. Did you forget there's a time limit?"

Shit. I did forget about the time limit. An hour to hit all seven checkpoints? I scramble after her and grab the handles of the wheelchair. "Let's go."

The first checkpoint we stop at is at the baseball field. Ash pulls a card and groans. I peer over her shoulder.

"Queen of hearts. Good card, dream girl."

"Face card!" Petal's husband, Orion, hollers before handing her a shot glass. Winter Falls' poker run rules dictate you drink a shot whenever you draw a king, queen, or jack. "Cheers!"

She downs the shot and grimaces before handing the glass back to him. "Jägermeister? You are a mean one." She points toward the high school. "Next stop, Jeeves!"

By the time we hit the sixth checkpoint, my knee is aching and it's hard not to limp. Ash weaving in the wheelchair, since she's had to drink shots at three of the previous five checkpoints, isn't helping.

I nod toward the hotdog stand Lennon, the owner of the *Electric Vibes* bar, has set up. "You're eating a hotdog before we continue to the next checkpoint."

"Ketchup and relish, please."

She must be feeling the booze if she's not fighting me. I leave her at a table to order our food. I notice Ash frowning at me upon my return. When my gaze meets hers, though, she smiles.

"Thanks for the food, Jeeves. You're a good valet."

I bow and hand her the hotdog. She doesn't scarf down the food the way I expect. She takes her time eating and checks her watch.

"I think we should skip the last checkpoint," she announces. "I already have a flush."

"Are you kidding? You won't win with a flush. Unless it's a royal flush?"

"It's not, but the shots are hitting me hard." She fans her face.

She was fine a few minutes ago. What's going on? "What's wrong?"

Her eyebrows fly off the top of her head. "What do you mean?"

I grunt.

"I'm not lying," she proclaims. When I continue to stare her down, she huffs. "Fine! I noticed you're limping, and I don't want you to push the wheelchair anymore. There. Are you happy?"

"You're worried I'm in pain?"

"Why do you sound surprised? Of course, I'm worried. I love you. I don't want you to be in pain. Your pain is my pain." She doesn't let me speak before rushing on. "Let's go turn in my hand and get you home." She wiggles her eyebrows. "I hear baths are wonderful for sore muscles."

I stand. "Nope. We're going to the last checkpoint."

"Rowan," she growls, "you're in pain."

"I'll be fine," I insist. "I'm not allowing you to lose. Not when I know how much it means to you to give the trip to a woman from the shelter."

She pats my hands. "It's okay, honey. I promise I'm not upset. Your health is more important."

I whirl the wheelchair around until she's facing me. "Do you promise to give me a rubdown when we get home?"

Her eyes brighten and her cheeks darken. "Whenever you want." Her voice comes out all breathy the same way it does when I'm moving inside her. My pants tighten and I clear my throat before I say screw it and accept what she's offering.

"Good. We're finishing this," I say before pushing the wheelchair and gathering speed.

Ash raises her hands in the air and screams, "I love you, Rowan Aries Hansley!"

I don't return the sentiment. Not because I don't love her, because I do. But I want the first time I tell her I love her to be a moment for her to remember. She deserves it after how I tortured her for the past year. She deserves the world and I plan to give it to her.

Chapter 34

Stumped – to be confused and/or surprised, which may cause a person to act like a complete and utter idiot

I SIT ON THE sofa and wait for Rowan to return home from work. I'm wearing a sweater dress and boots. Matching leather boots because someone got her cast off today! I can't wait to tell Rowan. Sexy times will be way more sexy when he doesn't grunt at me to put my boot back on the second he finishes climaxing. I wish I were exaggerating, but Rowan takes managing my recovery to the next level.

Rowan strolls into the house and I jump to my feet, but before I can shout ta-da, he's dashing toward me.

"Be careful. Jumping is bad for your ankle."

I push him away. "No, it isn't. Have a gander for yourself."

I begin marching around while doing high kicks. Maybe not high kicks. Who besides bubbly teenaged cheerleaders can do high kicks? Not this drama geek.

"You got your cast off?"

"Thank you, Captain Obvious."

I beam up at him, expecting him to pick me up and whirl me around, but he doesn't move. His lips turn down and his nose scrunches. What the hell?

My smile falters as I continue to stare at him. I can't read whatever emotion is swirling around in his eyes. Shit. Did I read this situation all wrong? I thought— I shake my head. It doesn't matter what I thought. This is not the happy ending I was expecting.

"I guess I'll go pack."

When Rowan still doesn't speak, my shoulders slump and I dash toward our bedroom – no! not *our* bedroom, Rowan's bedroom – before the tears can fall. I slam the door behind me and collapse against it. I rub my fists in my eyes. I will not cry. I will not let him see how devastated I am by his reaction.

With my tears successfully held at bay, I scurry around the room throwing all my things in my suitcase. I swipe the vanity in the bathroom and throw all my bits and bobbles in a trash bag. Five minutes later, I survey the room to make sure all remnants of my presence have been removed. They have. I swallow down my dismay at the thought of how easily I can be erased from Rowan's life and open the door.

Rowan's standing in the living room rubbing his neck. He raises his head when he hears me approach, but he can't look me in the eyes.

"Let me drive you home."

He jingles the keys to the golf cart, and I nab it from him. "Thanks. I'll return the cart later." Later as in when I damn well feel like it.

He doesn't stop me when I trudge out of his house and throw my things in the cart. In fact, he doesn't bother following me out of the house at all. What the hell? Was everything we said to each other a lie? Why is he acting this way? What happened? Is he done with me now he doesn't need to take care of me?

My breath hitches at all the thoughts rolling around in my brain, but I will not cry. At least, not yet. I switch on the golf cart and zoom away with my heart breaking the further away from Rowan's house I get.

I slam to a stop in front of my old apartment. The golf cart, which by the way, I'm not returning – if Rowan wants his cart back, he can darn well get off his ridiculously gorgeous ass and come get it – shutters as it stalls. I grab my things and stomp into the place I share with my sister.

I drop my bags inside the door before rushing up the stairs toward my bedroom. The first tear falls as I reach the top stair. By the time I make it to my bedroom, where I collapse face first on my bed, I'm all out bawling.

I don't know how long I lay there before someone knocks on my bedroom door. "Ash? Are you okay?" Juniper asks.

"What are you doing here?" I ask my pillow.

"Rowan messaged me. He thought you might be upset."

You have got to be kidding me. I roll over and jack-knife out of bed. "Might be upset?" I explode. "Might be upset!"

Juniper holds up her hands and backs away from me. "Whoa, zombie girl. Don't eat my brains."

"I'll eat more than your brains. I'll tear your hair out," I promise as I march toward her.

"Eek! Help!" she screams as she runs away.

I rush after her until we reach the living room where she hides behind Aspen. Unfortunately, Aspen's not alone. Ellery and Lilac are here, too.

"Awesome!" I throw my hands in the air. "It's always been my dream to have my sisters around to witness my heartbreak."

Aspen wraps her arms around me and sways me from side to side. I push her away. I'm not a child!

"Did you and Rowan break up?"

"Yes."

I mean, I assume we did. He stood there like a deaf mute after I announced my ankle was healed. And here I was thinking it was cause for celebration. I groan. Crap. I left a bottle of champagne chilling in his refrigerator. At least I'm not there to be mortified when he finds it.

"What happened?" Juniper asks as she takes my hand and leads me to the sofa.

I yank on her hand to stall her before she can push me down.

"Why is there a wet spot on the sofa?"

"You know Bark Twain hasn't been feeling well."

My nose wrinkles, and I retreat. "As in he's been throwing up on the sofa?"

Great. This is exactly the kind of welcome home I envisioned. Not.

"For goodness sakes." Lilac marches into the kitchen and returns with a towel. She places it on the wet spot before motioning for me to sit down.

I plunk down on the sofa and prop my legs on the coffee table.

"Yeah!" Juniper claps. "You got your cast off."

"You were supposed to have the cast on for another week." Lilac would know. Her brain is a holding tank for all the information in the world. "Why did you get it off early?"

"And why didn't you tell us?" Ellery asks.

"I know why," Aspen sings. I throw daggers out of my eyes at her, but she keeps right on talking as if my daggers are merely love bites instead of the weapons of steel destruction they actually are. "She wanted to surprise Rowan first."

"And look how that turned out," I grumble.

She plops down next to me and grasps my hand. "What happened?"

"Nothing."

She bumps my shoulder. "Come on. You can tell us. We know how to keep a secret."

"Really?" Ellery cocks an eyebrow. "The same way you kept it a secret when I skipped the school assembly?"

Aspen shrugs. "Better for you to get in trouble for skipping a stupid assembly than anyone find out about how I put hot sauce in Love Hill's tomato soup."

"Before we bring up every single wrong one of us has done to another of us, perhaps we could return to the matter at hand," Lilac suggests.

"As if you've ever been wronged," Ellery mumbles.

"I cannot help it if I was the perfect child."

Ellery's mouth drops open as she stares at Lilac. "Did you use sarcasm?"

Lilac's mouth purses. "Of course not. There's nothing ironic about my being the perfect child. It's simply a matter of fact."

Juniper fishes out her phone. "I'm calling Mom. We'll find out if she thinks you're the perfect child."

I slap the phone out of her hand and it crashes to the floor. The sound scares Dale who was sneaking onto the sofa and he titters as he sprints away.

Ellery screams and jumps onto the coffee table. "Don't let the critter bite me!"

Juniper ignores her to demand, "What's wrong with you?"

I point to my face. "Maybe I don't want to see Mom while I'm covered in mascara and snot."

"Okay." Aspen stands. "We need tequila, chocolate, and a romcom."

"I've got the perfect movie," Juniper declares before darting off.

Lilac lifts up her bag. "As instructed, I brought chocolate."

"I—"

I cut Aspen off. "Hold on. As instructed? Did Rowan the heart destroyer message all of my sisters to tell them I was heartbroken? Can he be more of an asshole?"

He couldn't talk to me about what's going on with him, but he could connect with my sisters to let them know he broke my heart? What the hell is wrong with the man? I should have believed him when he said he can't make a woman happy. Stupid foolish Ashlyn.

"Whatever you're thinking, stop," Aspen demands. "Rowan didn't say a word to us about you being heartbroken."

I narrow my eyes on her. "Rowan messaged Juniper to tell her I was upset," I remind her.

Her nose twitches signaling whatever's about to come out of her mouth is a lie. "But he didn't call us. And he never said anything about you being heartbroken."

I growl. I know she's lying. I open my mouth to berate her, but I snap it shut just as quickly again. What does it matter? Rowan's an asshole who doesn't love me. End of discussion.

Aspen squeezes my hand. "What are you thinking?"

"I'm thinking I never should have veered off the 'get over my crush on Rowan'-path I began before I broke my ankle," I say and promptly burst into tears.

"We need tequila stat!" Aspen hollers.

Ellery backs away. "Don't look at me. I'm not drinking. I have to work in the morning."

"And?" Aspen pushes. "You don't get hangovers."

"I don't care if Ellery drinks," I wail. "But I need about fifty shots to make me forget what a fool I am for thinking the man I've loved since I was an idiot teenager loves me back."

"Oh, Ash." Juniper plops down on the other side of me and throws her arms around me. "You're not a fool. If Rowan can't see what a treasure he has in you, he's the fool."

"Here." Aspen shoves a shot glass in front of my face. "Drink. There's nothing tequila, chocolate, and a funny movie can't cure."

Easy for her to say. She's going home to the man she's loved since she was in kindergarten while I'll probably live with Juniper and her thousand animals until I die. Meowise hisses before she claws at my boots. Great. My journey to spinster cat lady has already begun.

Chapter 35

Quarterback – one who often thinks he's a mastermind

ROWAN

I pace in front of *Naked Falls Brewing* as I wait for Ash to arrive. Aspen promised she would bring Ash here today, but I'm not sure how she'll manage it. Ash doesn't go anywhere she doesn't want to, and she doesn't want to be anywhere near me at the moment.

I can't blame her. I completely blanked when she announced her ankle was healed. She wasn't supposed to have her cast off until next week. I thought I had more time to prepare my surprise. Instead, Ash surprised me, and I went mute.

By the time my brain caught up to what was happening, Ash was barreling away on my golf cart with all her things. I hadn't intended to ever let her leave – regardless of the condition of her ankle – but I did. I'm such an idiot.

"Stop pacing!" Bryan hisses at me. "You're making me nervous."

I scan the crowd gathered and wonder if I've completely lost my mind. Why didn't I tell Ash I loved her when we were alone? What made me think this was a good idea?"

"Your face went all scrunchy. You need to stop whatever crazy thoughts are in your brain this minute."

"I—"

The words get caught in my throat when I catch sight of Ash. She's obviously unhappy about being here. Good. Aspen didn't give away the surprise. Or, maybe she did, and Ash won't forgive me and thinks I'm a fool.

Ash's gaze finds mine and she freezes. She tries to back away, but Lilac blocks her while Juniper captures her hand and drags her to me.

"You owe me," Juniper says as she deposits Ash in front of me.

"What's going on?" Ash asks as she scans the crowd of spectators. "Why is the entire town of Winter Falls here?"

I thought I was nervous the first time I was chosen to play first string in an NFL game. But those nerves were nothing compared to how I feel now. If Ash doesn't forgive me, I don't know how I'll go on. But I'm not going to find out if I stand here speechless. I should know better after yesterday.

"Ash, may I take your hands?" I begin.

Her nose wrinkles. "You're asking to touch me? What's going on?"

"I can't do this if I'm not touching you," I whisper my admission to her.

She rolls her eyes, but she also holds her hands out to me. I cling to them.

"Ashlyn Dream West, I love you." The words slip out. I didn't intend to begin my grand gesture by declaring my love, but I can't stand her not knowing how I feel for another second.

"But you let me leave yesterday. Why didn't you ask me to stay?"

"Because you surprised me. Because I had a flashback of Sandra walking away when I was in the hospital."

She gasps before her eyes spit daggers at me. "Don't you dare compare me to your ex-wife ever again. You hear me. You think Aspen shaving Lyric's entire freaking body when she was mad at him was bad? You ain't seen nothing yet."

I bite my lip to stop my smile from emerging. My little spitfire would not appreciate my amusement at her threats. I incline my head. "I will never compare you to Sandra again," I vow.

"Good. You may proceed."

This is supposed to be my show, but somehow Ash is running it. I might as well get used to it. This woman is going to run roughshod over my life and I'm happy to let her. No, more than happy. I'm fucking ecstatic.

"I'm sorry. I'm sorry I let you leave yesterday. It's one of the biggest regrets of my life."

Her eyes narrow as she studies me. I let her see all the emotions I'm feeling. I don't hide a single thing from her. After what feels like an eternity, she nods.

"I forgive you. But you better not go mute on me again, you hear? If you need time to think, you tell me, and I'll give it to you. Nod if you understand."

I chuckle. "I understand. Now, do you want to see your surprise?"

She taps her chin and pretends to think about it. She isn't fooling me. I can see her bouncing on her toes in excitement. Finally, she shrugs. "I guess."

I grasp her hand and tug her next door. There's a red ribbon in front of the door to the previously empty storefront, and Forest is waiting for us with the ceremonial scissors.

Ash narrows her gaze on me. "What's this? What's going on?"

I haul her into the alley between the two stores. "This is your big surprise."

"I thought the whole 'I love you' was my big surprise."

I snort. "Not hardly," I say but don't elaborate.

She wrenches her hand from mine to cross her arms over her chest. "Are you going to tell me what this big surprise is?"

"I'd prefer to show you."

"This better not be you making big decisions without my input again."

I cringe. Unfortunately, Ash notices. "I can see the future and, trust me, you're in big trouble."

Since her voice is full of humor, I decide it's time to get the show on the road. I tag her hand and lead her to the front of the store where Forest is still waiting.

"Gosh darn it," Petal huffs as she hands Sage a five-dollar bill. "I hate losing bets."

Sage giggles. "You didn't honestly think they were going to make love in a dirty alley, did you?"

I groan and speak to Forest in a loud voice to avoid hearing the rest of whatever the Gossip Gals are going to say. "We're ready."

"Ashlyn Dream West. Front and center," he commands.

Ash shakes her head at me before joining him.

"Proud of you, baby girl," Mr. West shouts while Mrs. West blows her a kiss.

Forest clears his throat. "If we can get this show on the road now?"

Mrs. West motions for him to go ahead.

Forest places Ash's hand through one finger ring while he places his hand through the other. Together, they open the scissors and place the blades around the red ribbon.

"I now declare *Bertie's Recording Studio* open," Forest announces as the two cut through the ribbon.

The crowd cheers and pushes forward, but Ash is frozen where she is. I unclench her hand from the scissors and hand them to Forest before wrapping an arm around her waist and steering her toward the doors.

"Let's go check out your studio," I tell her.

"My studio?" she squeaks.

"Yep."

We enter the building, and she gasps. The interior has been completely transformed into a place that invites creativity. Directly in front of us is the reception area. In addition to the reception desk, there are several black, leather sofas for lounging. Off to the side is a bar area with a coffee counter and a fully stocked bar. In the rear are two recording booths.

Each booth has glass walls allowing anyone in the building to see inside the booths.

The booths are decked out with all the necessary recording equipment. I won't pretend I have a clue what any of it is. I contacted a friend from my football days, and he helped me order what I needed. It's all top of the line.

"This is crazy," Ash whispers as she surveys the area.

I lead her to the furthest booth. "Let me show you how the interior looks."

"I can't possibly afford all of this. What is the rent on this place going to cost?"

As if I'd ever let her pay rent. "You're not paying rent." She glares at me, but I cut her off before she can protest. "This is a joint venture between me and you. You'll operate the business while I'm the silent financial partner. It's all above board. My lawyer wrote up the contracts. But I don't want to talk about the legalese now."

"You don't?" she asks as she twirls around the booth to take it all in. Her movements halt and she bites her lip.

I close and lock the door before moving to her and taking her hands. "What is it? What's wrong? Do you not like it?"

She mumbles something, but her voice is too soft for me to hear.

I lean down to ask, "What did you say?"

Her gaze meets mine. "What if I fail?"

It's not even a consideration for me. "You won't."

"I have no idea how to run a recording studio. I'm just an audiobook narrator."

"Just?" I snort. "You, Ashlyn Dream West, are not just anything. You are amazing. You can succeed at anything you put your mind to. I admire your determination."

She rolls her eyes.

I squeeze her hands. "No. Don't be dismissive. I'm being honest here. You worked a million different jobs over the past year in order to make your business of being an audiobook narrator succeed. If you put that kind of determination into making the studio work, you can't fail."

She avoids my gaze to contemplate the floor. "I'm scared," she tells the floor.

I release her hands to cradle her face. I use my hold to lift her head until we're eye to eye. "Dream girl, I promise I won't let you fail."

She holds my gaze for several moments before speaking, "We're partners? Fifty/fifty?"

"Yes," I tell her.

She blows out a breath before nodding. "Okay. I'm in."

I feel my smile stretch from ear to ear before I kiss her forehead. She pushes up on her toes to reach my mouth, but I drop to my knee.

She gasps. "What are you doing?"

I dig in my pocket for the ring before extending my hand to show it to her. "Isn't it obvious?"

The vulnerable woman is nowhere to be seen as she crosses her arms and taps her toe. "Let's hear it."

I chuckle. "Ashlyn Dream West, will you marry me and become my dream wife for the rest of my life?"

"Yes," she screams and launches herself at me.

I wrap my arms around her as we fall back on the floor.

Knock. Knock. "Are you having hanky-panky?" Petal asks through the glass. "Let me go find Sage. I want my money back."

Ash sighs. "I love this town."

I kiss her nose. "And I love you."

Chapter 36

Low blow – an unfair attack

ELLERY

With everyone admiring Ashlyn's new studio, it's time for me to make my escape. Before I can retreat a single step, Aspen latches onto my upper arm.

"Where do you think you're going?"

I force myself to roll my eyes. "Back to work. Where else would I be going?"

"I wouldn't know since you're obviously keeping a secret from me."

She sounds hurt, and I waver on continuing to keep my secret. Maybe I should tell her. It would be nice to have someone to confide in.

"What are we talking about?" Juniper asks as she sidles up to Aspen. Her gaze bounces back and forth between the two of us and her forehead scrunches. "What's wrong?'

"Nothing's wrong," I'm quick to say.

Aspen's face flashes with pain and I feel like the biggest bitch in the history of mankind, which is saying a lot since I met Rowan's ex-wife.

"I need to get back to the inn." I lie.

I don't need to be at the inn nearly as much as I've claimed these past three months, but there's no way I can keep my secret if I'm around my sisters all the time. They'd sniff out my problem in no time. I'm convinced Aspen was a bloodhound in a previous life.

"You do?" Aspen cocks a brow. "I happen to know every single one of your clients is here celebrating the grand opening of Ashlyn's new studio."

"What's with the name Bertie's anyway?" Juniper asks. "Is it some inside joke between the two of them? I hope he doesn't call her Bertie in bed. Yuck."

"I think it's a reference to Bertie Wooster from the P.G. Woodhouse stories," Lilac answers as she joins us.

Aspen's jaw falls open. "You know who P.G. Woodhouse is?"

Lilac frowns. "Naturally. Don't you remember the play *Jeeves and Wooster in Perfect Nonsense* Ashlyn was in when she was in college? We went to see it together."

Aspen snaps her fingers. "Of course. I forgot."

"Anyway, why are you all standing here in the corner?" Lilac scans the room. "Shouldn't we be celebrating Ashlyn's engagement with her?"

Aspen snorts. "I think Ashlyn and Rowan want to celebrate their engagement alone." She gestures toward the emergency exit of the building where the two are currently sneaking off.

"I guess she forgives him for being an ass yesterday," I mumble.

"Duh. She's been in love with him forever. Naturally, she forgives him. It doesn't hurt he told her he loves her in front of the whole town before presenting her with a complete recording studio and proposing to her." Juniper sighs. "Some men know how to do romance."

Aspen smiles as her gaze locks on Lyric as he saunters into the building in his police uniform. "They certainly do."

I freeze when I notice who's behind Lyric. Shit. What is *he* doing here? I plaster myself to the wall and start slipping sideways toward the emergency exit. The place is packed. Maybe he won't notice me.

Aspen blocks my path. "Nope. You're not fleeing to hide at the inn until you tell us your secret."

"I don't hide at the inn."

"Tell it to someone who believes you."

"Are we referring to Ellery being pregnant?" Lilac asks.

While Juniper and Aspen gasp, I glare at Lilac. "How do you know?"

"It wasn't difficult to puzzle out. You haven't been drinking and you've been feeling nauseous a lot."

"I never said I was feeling nauseous."

Lilac sighs. "You don't have to say it for it to be true. It was obvious."

And here I thought I was hiding my condition from everyone.

"Can we not talk about this here?" I hiss. I don't want the entire town knowing. Not until I decide how I'm going to handle the situation.

Lilac studies me. "You won't be able to hide your pregnancy much longer. You'll begin showing soon."

Behind her, someone inhales sharply. I close my eyes and allow my head to fall back against the wall. This is not how I intended for him to find out.

"You're pregnant," Cole grumbles. "Is it mine?"

Before I can respond, my sisters are ushering me out of the building while Lyric herds Cole outside with us. They push us into the alley between the brewery and the recording studio.

"You don't have much time before the natives get restless," Lyric says before positioning himself at the mouth of the alley to guard our privacy.

I whirl on Cole. "How dare you ask if it's yours? Do you think I'm some kind of slut who sleeps with all her guests? If that's what you think, you can leave this minute."

He rubs a hand down his face. "I'm sorry. You shocked me. I don't think you're a slut." He pauses. "It's true? You're pregnant?"

I feel tears well in my eyes as I nod. "Yeah. I'm pregnant."

About Author

D.E. Haggerty is an American who has spent the majority of her adult life abroad. She has lived in Istanbul, various places throughout Germany, and currently finds herself in The Hague. She has been a military policewoman, a lawyer, a B&B owner/operator and now a writer.

Printed in Dunstable, United Kingdom